HIDDEN AGENDA

HIDDEN AGENDA

M A COMLEY

2018

New York Times and USA Today bestselling author M A Comley
Published by Jeamel Publishing limited
Copyright © 2018 M A Comley
Digital Edition, License Notes

All rights reserved. This book or any portion thereof may not be reproduced, stored in a retrieval system, transmitted in any form or by any means electronic or mechanical, including photo-copying, or used in any manner whatsoever without the express written permission of the author, except for the use of brief quotations in a book review or scholarly journal.

This is a work of fiction. Names, characters, places and incidents are a product of the author's imagination or are used fictitiously, and any resemblance to actual persons living or dead, business establishments, events or locales is entirely coincidental.

ISBN-13: 978-1985711891

ISBN-10: 1985711893

In loving memory of my biggest fan and dearest friend for the last seven years. R.I.P. Mary Endersbe. I will miss our daily chats, your gentle nature and your warm smile. Until we meet again...

OTHER BOOKS BY M A COMLEY

Blind Justice (Novella)
Cruel Justice (Book #1)
Mortal Justice (Novella)
Impeding Justice (Book #2)
Final Justice (Book #3)
Foul Justice (Book #4)
Guaranteed Justice (Book #5)
Ultimate Justice (Book #6)
Virtual Justice (Book #7)
Hostile Justice (Book #8)
Tortured Justice (Book #9)
Rough Justice (Book #10)
Dubious Justice (Book #11)
Calculated Justice (Book #12)
Twisted Justice (Book #13)
Justice at Christmas (Short Story)
Prime Justice (Book #14)
Heroic Justice (Book #15)
Shameful Justice (Book #16 coming May 2018)
Unfair Justice (a 10,000 word short story)
Irrational Justice (a 10,000 word short story)
Clever Deception (co-written by Linda S Prather)
Tragic Deception (co-written by Linda S Prather)
Sinful Deception (co-written by Linda S Prather)
Forever Watching You (DI Miranda Carr thriller)
Wrong Place (DI Sally Parker thriller #1)
No Hiding Place (DI Sally Parker thriller #2)
Cold Case (DI Sally Parker #3)

Deadly Encounter (DI Sally Parker thriller series #4)
Web of Deceit (DI Sally Parker Novella with Tara Lyons)
The Missing Children (DI Kayli Bright #1)
Killer On The Run (DI Kayli Bright #2)
Hidden Agenda (DI Kayli Bright #3)
The Caller (co-written with Tara Lyons)
Evil In Disguise – a novel based on True events
Deadly Act (Hero series novella)
Torn Apart (Hero series #1)
End Result (Hero series #2)
In Plain Sight (Hero Series #3)
Double Jeopardy (Hero Series #4)
Sole Intention (Intention series #1)
Grave Intention (Intention series #2)
Devious Intention (Intention #3)
Merry Widow (A Lorne Simpkins short story)
It's A Dog's Life (A Lorne Simpkins short story)
A Time To Heal (A Sweet Romance)
A Time For Change (A Sweet Romance)
High Spirits
The Temptation series (Romantic Suspense/New Adult Novellas)
Past Temptation (available now)
Lost Temptation (available now)

KEEP IN TOUCH WITH THE AUTHOR:

Twitter
https://twitter.com/Melcom1

Blog
http://melcomley.blogspot.com

Facebook
http://smarturl.it/sps7jh

Newsletter
http://smarturl.it/8jtcvv

BookBub
www.bookbub.com/authors/m-a-comley

ACKNOWLEDGMENTS

Thank you as always to my rock, Jean, who keeps me supplied with endless cups of coffee while I punish my keyboard. I'd be lost without you in my life.

Special thanks as always go to my talented editor, Stefanie Spangler Buswell and to Karri Klawiter for her superb cover design expertise.

My heartfelt thanks go to my wonderful proofreader Joseph for spotting all the lingering nits.

Thank you also to Kayli and Donna from my ARC group for allowing me to use your names in this novel.

I'd also like to say a very special thank you to two people who can't be named, who shared their valuable expertise in the field of overseas security procedures with me.

And finally, to all the wonderful Bloggers and Facebook groups for their never-ending support of my work.

Hidden Agenda

PROLOGUE

Sarah breathed a relieved sigh as she dropped into the passenger seat of Danny's car. It was the end of a very long week at the radio station where she worked alongside Danny. She was one of the people who worked behind the scenes, writing the DJs' scripts. She loved her job, but every now and then, a DJ's barbed, sarcastic jibe got to her. If they weren't slapping her backside as she passed, they were making lewd and improper comments about her larger-than-average breasts. She had complained to her male boss numerous times in the last few months alone, but he had just waved away her complaints, telling her she should accept that it was part of the job.

For over a year, she'd been on the lookout for a new job within the industry she loved, but no one seemed to be hiring. With Brexit looming ever nearer, the economy was so unstable that employers feared a recession was inevitable.

Danny was different from the others, though. He was thoughtful and considerate, and he always treated her like a lady whenever she was within earshot. She'd never heard him speak in a derogatory manner towards any of his female colleagues. He just wasn't like that. With her car in the garage for repairs, Sarah had mentioned needing to get a taxi home from work, and Danny had graciously offered to give her a lift. His kindness meant that Sarah didn't have to wait in a long queue to hop on a bus. Plus, she hated all forms of public transport.

He slipped behind the steering wheel and smiled. "Sorry about that. Tim wanted a final word on the project we've been working on."

"No problem. Thanks again for giving me a lift home, Danny. I know it's going out of your way. I feel guilty about that, but appreciative nonetheless."

He waved a hand in front of him. "It's only a few minutes out of the way. I'm happy to lend a hand when I can. You know that.

No idea what the traffic is going to be like on your side of town at this time of night, though."

"It should be okay." At five twenty, the traffic was usually beginning to die down from the manic rush hour. She hoped that was the case this evening because she hated to think she'd delayed Danny too much after his kind gesture. "Any plans for this evening?"

"Not really. I'll pick up a takeaway on the way home and settle down to a few cans of beer whilst listening to a few albums, I suppose. Same old thing. What about you?"

"What would you men do without having a takeaway of choice available on every conceivable corner? Me? I'm going to have a long soak in the bath with a bottle of wine and heat up a portion of chicken casserole I had yesterday. Exciting, right?"

They both chuckled. "It's about as exciting as my life gets. No man on the scene at the moment then, Sarah?"

"No. Not since I kicked Gary out a few months ago. I'm better off alone, if I'm honest. Only having myself to answer to when I want to do something. I really don't understand why people have to change so much when they enter into a relationship. Do you?"

Danny paused before answering. "I've never really thought about it before. It's been a while since I've been in that predicament."

Sarah laughed. "Predicament? Never thought of a relationship in those terms before. You know what? I think you're right—you're spot-on, in fact. A relationship is more like a predicament than a genuine coming together of minds. It's very rare that people don't have to make sacrifices when they enter into a relationship with a partner. I think that gets even worse once a wedding ring is slipped on your finger. Oh gosh—hark at me! Sorry for boring you with my ideas. Not everyone analyses life like I do."

"I think it's refreshing to hear different people's perspectives on things: life, relationships, work. Go for it. Talking about work, did you get that nasty business with Ryan sorted?"

Sarah fell quiet before she answered, "As sorted as it's going to be, I guess. I suspect the boss thought I was exaggerating a bit. I suppose Ryan is the big star at work, and I'm just a menial compared to him. I can understand the boss taking his word in that instance."

Danny struck the steering wheel with the heel of his hand. "That's so unfair. What the hell is Harry thinking about? You have a voice and deserve to be heard. Crap, you'd think everyone would be more vigilant in our business after all the high-profile sex charges that have been highlighted in recent years. Oh God, listen to me. I'm sorry for sounding so angry. It just really pisses me off that cretins like Ryan can treat women so appallingly and get away with it."

Sarah placed her hand over his. "Thank you for defending women's honour so vehemently. Lord knows what would happen if the tables were turned and women started sexually harassing men at work. Actually, scrub that. I reckon you guys would be in your element, lapping up all the attention." Sarah laughed.

"I fear you could be right about that. Strange, isn't it? The gender differences, I mean. When a girl is harassed, they scream blue murder, and when a bloke is touched up by a woman, he revels in it, deeming it to mean that his luck is in."

"You know the saying about men being from Mars? I happen to think that's a fair analogy. We are totally different, and anyone who denies that needs their head read in my opinion. Sorry, take the next on the right. My flat is halfway down the street."

"I do think you have something there. Looking at my own mother and father's relationship—crikey! That would be enough to put off anyone who was considering diving into marriage. Maybe that's why I'm still single at thirty."

Sarah smiled. "Nah, you just haven't met the right person to settle down with yet. You will, one day. I'm confident about that."

"I'm glad you are." He smiled, pulling up outside the semi-detached house which was divided into two flats.

"Thanks so much, Danny. You've been a lifesaver. Well, maybe that was a tad over the top, but you know what I mean."

"Maybe we could go out with a drink after work sometime?"

She leaned over to kiss his cheek then left the vehicle, bending down she said, "You're such a sweet guy, to be honest with you, I think there's every chance Gary and I might get back together." *I hope he doesn't realise I'm lying, not sure I'm ready to start dating again just yet.*

"No worries. See you Monday," he shouted before she slammed the car door shut.

Sarah stood in the glare of the streetlight, gave him the thumbs-up, and waved him off before she ran up the steps to her front door. Letting herself in, she shuddered in the hallway. The house dated back to the 1930s, and the hall felt chilly as she walked its length to the kitchen. The cost of heating the place was exorbitant, so she and her flatmate, Jane, had agreed they would only put the heating on once they were both at home for a few hours in the evening. Jane, a nurse on a women's ward, was due home in an hour or so.

Entering the kitchen, Sarah made a beeline for the gas cooker. She lit the large front burner and hovered her hands over it for a few minutes, until the warmth penetrated her body. Then she walked through to the bathroom to run a bath. Thinking she'd caught a motion near the front door, she halted in the hallway. Realising what she'd thought was the outline of a person was only shadow, Sarah shook her head.

In the bathroom, she poured a big dollop of lavender foam bath into the tub. She walked into her bedroom to gather her pyjamas and towelling robe, which she deposited in the bathroom before returning to the kitchen where she filled a glass from a newly opened bottle of Chardonnay.

The next fifteen minutes were spent in the bath, sipping her glass of wine and listening to a Bee Gees CD she'd dug out of her collection. *I better get out before I start resembling a dried prune.* After towelling herself dry, she dipped into her bedroom to blow-dry her hair. Unsure whether she heard the doorbell ring or not, she switched off the hairdryer and tilted her head. Then it rang again.

"God, what is it now? Some Jehovah's Witness or someone else just as annoying, no doubt." Tightening her robe, she called out, "Just a minute!"

She opened the door, only to find no one was there. Tutting loudly, she began to close it again, but before the door could reach the jamb, someone jumped out from the shadows and rammed it open. She toppled backwards with the force, banging the back of her head on the wooden dado rail halfway up the wall. Her head instantly felt as though it belonged to someone else, and her vision became virtually non-existent as she felt the intruder gather her into his arms. She heard him muttering how beautiful she was before the front door slammed and he flicked the catch to lock it.

Weakly, she attempted to wriggle out of his arms, but bile crept into her mouth. Unable to contain the contents of her stomach, she vomited over her intruder and heard him curse. He wound his way through the flat to her bedroom and threw her on the bed. Frustration rose from her toes as she tried to sit up several times, failing and falling back against her pillow each time. Feeling vulnerable, she was desperate to secure her robe around her middle, but her limbs failed to cooperate, and she couldn't locate the belt. *My God, why is he doing this? I have to get out of here.*

"Relax. You're going to enjoy this." His singsong voice confused her.

She had to put up some kind of fight, but the room was spinning, the man's image was a blur, and she constantly felt as though she was going to vomit again. Her arms and legs felt like they didn't belong to her, either. *If there truly is a God up there, please help me.*

His torso blocked out the light above, and she blinked several times, trying to clear her vision. Then she felt him tugging at the buttons on her pyjamas. She closed her eyes as if summoning up enough strength to begin her fight. She screamed, long and hard, hoping this would deter him. If anything, his hands became more violent in their mission.

For the first time, she noticed he was wearing a mask, a balaclava. "Please, please, don't hurt me. I have money. Take my credit card! I'll give you the PIN number. I have a couple of thousand in the bank. It's yours—just please don't hurt me." Even to her own ears, her words sounded slurred.

His laugh ridiculed her words. "It's not your money I want. It's *you*."

"Please... please don't do anything that you'll regret," she begged, her voice sounding distant.

His hand struck her face. She yelped as the pain sent a message to her fuzzy mind that he'd struck her. She didn't have the strength to fight him. Her limbs appeared to have a life of their own, otherwise she would have kicked out at him or kneed him in the groin, as her self-defence instructor had told her to do in such circumstances. Instead of finding the strength to fight him off, she succumbed to an overwhelming tiredness.

"Please, I'm begging you, don't do this," she mumbled.

He laughed again and proceeded to tug at her clothes. Her legs and arms went in the opposite direction to where she intended them to go. She felt hopeless and helpless against this man who seemed to be blessed with super-human strength.

The tiredness subsided once more, long enough for her to think of Jane. "My flatmate, she's going to be home anytime."

He paused for a moment before he pulled her upright and forced her arms behind her back. The quick movement made her head swim.

He tied her hands with a plastic tie and tightened it, pinching the skin on her wrist, causing her to cry out.

"Please, you're hurting me."

"Stop whining. If you think this is hurting you, then you're gravely mistaken."

She saw his arm move and flinched but then realised he was looking at his watch. Maybe her warning about Jane would be the one thing to save her. She heard a rustling noise, then a plastic bag covered her face.

She gasped. "No, please. I can't breathe. Don't do this. Take what you want and leave. I won't tell the police, I promise."

"You're right—you won't. Because dead people can't speak," he sneered against her ear. He tightened his grip around the bag, cutting off the air.

Unable to hold back any longer, she vomited. As the foul liquid filled the bag, her panic set in. She twisted her body, trying to get her hands out of her bindings and the bag off her head. The smell of her own vomit made her heave as she fought for her breath. His laughter was the last thing Sarah heard as she sank into oblivion.

CHAPTER ONE

Detective Inspector Kayli Bright received the call on her way home from work. "Yes, I'll attend. Can you ring DS Dave Chaplin? Get him to meet me at the location."

"I'll ring him now, ma'am. Thank you."

Kayli stopped the car, reversed into someone's drive, and headed back into the city of Bristol. Her thoughts turned to solving the crime of the poor woman whose body had just been discovered in her own home. That was all the information Kayli had so far.

Fifteen minutes later, Kayli found a parking space close to the victim's address. She opened the boot of her car, extracted a white forensic suit, and pulled it on. After slipping a pair of plastic shoes over her ankle boots, she snapped on a pair of blue latex gloves. A uniformed officer was guarding the front door. Kayli flashed him her ID. "DI Bright, SIO on the case. Don't let anyone else in until I say they can come in, okay?"

"Yes, ma'am. The victim is in the bedroom."

"Thanks. Any witnesses? Who called it in?"

He pointed to a young woman sitting on a nearby wall, bawling her eyes out as she gave a statement to a young uniformed female officer.

"Can you ask your colleague to get the witness's statement down inside her vehicle? It's cold, and she's probably suffering from shock as it is. Use your common sense and get that actioned immediately," Kayli snapped.

The officer rushed down the steps and whispered something in his partner's ear. The female officer looked Kayli's way and nodded, then the pair of them accompanied the young woman to their car and placed her in the back seat. Satisfied, Kayli entered the house. She walked through the rooms, one by one, making mental notes. There was a handbag on the kitchen table—did that belong to the victim or the witness? She followed the smell of lavender into the bathroom, where the remains of what appeared to have been bubble bath circled the tub's plughole. The small window was open, and there was a muddy footprint on the edge of the bath. Did the assailant enter the window, or was that the way he escaped the crime scene?

Hearing someone call her name, she retreated into the hallway to find her partner, Dave Chaplin, hobbling through the door on his crutches. "Stop! You know better than that, matey. Get togged up. You can't come in here like that." She suddenly felt guilty about calling him out to the scene, since he was struggling with a broken leg. Still, he *had* insisted since his 'accident' that she treat him as normal.

He let out an exasperated breath, turned, and headed back to his car. Dave reappeared a few moments later wearing an outfit identical to hers, a crutch tucked under each arm.

"Sorry, matey. You're hindered enough at the moment with those things. Come with me. I'm walking the scene."

"I'm used to them. It's a slight inconvenience. That's all. Have you seen the vic yet?"

"Not yet. Looks like her handbag is untouched in the kitchen, although that could be the witness's bag. Apparently, her flatmate was the one who found her. She's out there now, giving a statement to uniform." Kayli led Dave into the bathroom and pointed out the muddy footprint.

"Point of entry or escape route?" Dave asked. He leaned in to observe the print more closely. "All right, the shape of the print and the amount of mud on the surface of the bath indicates it's an entry point to me."

Kayli smiled and nodded. "Good spot."

"The vic is in the bedroom. That's our next port of call." She pushed open the door opposite the bathroom and froze. The victim, a young woman, was sitting upright on the bed. Though dishevelled, she was still wearing her pyjamas and robe, although some of the buttons on her pjs were undone.

Kayli swallowed the bile burning her throat. "Jesus." Her gaze latched on to the woman's head, which was trapped in a plastic bag half-filled with the woman's own vomit.

Dave dry heaved. "Oh, fuck! That's gross."

"She either suffocated or drowned in her own vomit. We won't know until Naomi has had a chance to examine her. Appalling death, either way. Poor woman."

Dave navigated the room to stand on the other side of the bed. He bent down to look at the woman's hands, which were behind her. "She was tied up. Wait a minute... look." He pointed to the back of the victim's head. "Blood."

Kayli's eyes narrowed as she thought. "Maybe she was struck over the head first and tied up while she was unconscious. A head injury might have caused her to vomit."

"DI Bright?" Naomi called out from the main door. "Are you here?"

"Hi, Naomi. We're in the bedroom."

Naomi Stacy, the resident pathologist in the Bristol area, poked her head into the room. "Ugh... that's not pretty."

"Tell me about it. Thanks for dropping everything and coming over. We've got a muddy footprint in the bathroom. Dave reckons that was the way the assailant entered the premises."

"My guys are just sorting out the equipment now. I'll get them on that right away in case it disappears. Anything else I should know?" She placed her case on the floor at the foot of the bed.

"A handbag in the kitchen. Now I've seen the victim, I'm going to see if there is any ID inside. It might belong to the witness outside, the vic's flatmate."

"You do that while I carry out a quick assessment."

Kayli motioned for Dave to join her in the kitchen. She opened the handbag and dipped her hand inside to find the woman's purse. She found her driving licence and studied the woman's photo. "Ah, here we are. Sarah Abel. That's definitely her. Shit, she's only twenty-six." Kayli shook her head, upset for both the victim and the family yet to be informed. "I could do with Donna being on duty back at the station right now. She'd have the woman's next of kin within seconds."

"I'll ring her. She won't mind returning to work if it's for a good cause. The media are already sniffing around outside. If they start airing the residence, it could be distressing for the family to see it on TV."

"You're right. Ring her, Dave. Send her my apologies, but tell her it's important."

Dave punched Donna's number into his phone and put it on speaker when she answered. "Donna, we need your expertise on a new case. Any chance you can get back to the station?"

"Of course. I can be there in ten minutes. What do you need, Dave?"

"Next of kin on a Sarah Abel, of Fifty-two Winchester Avenue, in the Saint Paul's area."

"On it. I'll get the info to you ASAP," Donna replied.

"Thanks, Donna. I really appreciate it. You know how important the golden hour is in an investigation," Kayli shouted.

"I do, boss. Leave it with me."

"You're a star, Donna. Speak soon," Dave said before he hung up.

"I need to have a quick chat with Naomi first, and then I think we should see what the witness has to say." They walked through to the bedroom again to find two other members of Naomi's team in the room with her. One was taking photos of the victim from several angles. "Any idea about the cause of death yet, Naomi?"

"Hmm... hard to tell. Could be suffocation or drowning at this stage. I'll know more when I open her up and inspect her airways et cetera. Either way, she suffered a ghastly death."

"Did you notice the wound on the back of her head?"

"I did. I also noticed blood on the dado rail just inside the front door on my way in too."

Kayli groaned. "Damn, I missed that."

"Therefore, I'm assuming either the assailant came through the front door, or the victim ran towards the front door, trying to escape. My take is that she opened the door to her assailant, he surprised her, and either jumped out on her or shoved her back. She lost her footing and hit her head on the dado rail on the way down. Either way, the force wasn't enough to kill her. Because she vomited in the bag, we know she wasn't dead before it was placed over her head."

"I like your thinking. Seems plausible to me," Kayli said.

"I need to process the scene. Is there anything else you need to know before I get on with doing that?" Naomi asked.

"Nope. We'll let you get on. I want to question the witness now anyway. Let me know the results as soon as you can."

"I will. Don't worry."

Kayli and Dave made their way back to Kayli's car, where they stripped off their protective clothing.

"The witness looks really upset. I hope we get some sense out of her," Kayli said. She reached out and gave Dave a helping hand with his crutches.

"That's natural, I guess, after coming home from work and finding your flatmate dead."

"All right, Dave, stop stating the obvious."

Balancing on one leg, he smiled tautly as he tugged off the final leg of his suit and discarded it. Kayli picked up both suits and slung them in the boot of her car. "Let's do this."

She tapped on the window of the patrol vehicle. The startled young PC opened the door and got out. "Sorry, ma'am. I'm just winding up here."

"That's okay, Constable. We'd like a word with the witness as soon as we can."

"Do you want to use my car, ma'am?"

"Thanks, I'll hop in the back. My partner can sit up front." Kayli opened the back door, slid in the seat, and smiled at the blonde woman, who was shaking, despite her thick woollen black winter coat. "Hello, Jane. I'm DI Kayli Bright, the officer in charge of the case, and this is my partner, DS Dave Chaplin."

Dave waved his hand and pulled his broken leg into the car before he shut the door.

The young woman sniffled and muttered, "Why? Why Sarah?"

"We don't know yet. But it's our intention to find out. What time did you arrive home?"

"At just gone six thirty, my usual time."

"Did you see anyone in the property when you arrived?"

Jane shook her head. "No. The front door was locked. My key wouldn't turn, so I couldn't get in."

Kayli glanced at Dave then back at the witness. "So, how did you gain access to the property?"

"I climbed in through the bathroom window. Sarah and I had an agreement to always leave it open in case one of us forgets the key."

"That means the muddy footprint on the side of the bath was yours then?"

"Yes, I didn't think to wipe my feet before entering."

Kayli couldn't tell if the comment was sarcasm or shock, so she ignored it. "Did you try the front door once you got inside?"

"Yes, someone had dropped the latch on the front door."

Dave looked up from his notebook. "Is it usual for Sarah to drop the latch once she's home?"

"No. We never usually do that until the end of the evening, before we go to bed."

"Have either you or Sarah had any problems with anyone lately? Either of you have boyfriends?"

"I have a boyfriend, Sonny. He's on holiday with friends in the US at the moment. Sarah split up with her latest fella, Gary, a few months ago."

"Gary? Do you know his surname?" Kayli asked, her heart rate notching up a little.

"Gary Young. He's in the navy, down in Plymouth."

"When was the last time Sarah saw Gary, do you know?"

"A few weeks ago. He came home on leave for the weekend, called round to see how she was. They were still pretty friendly with each other, although she let it slip he struck out at her once. They just found the distance between them unacceptable to have a lasting relationship. My God, he's going to be gutted when he hears about poor Sarah." She shook her head, and fresh tears ran down her cheeks. "What am I going to do without her? We were like sisters. Shared all our secrets and celebrated all our successes together."

"I'm so sorry. Can you tell us where Sarah worked?" Kayli rubbed the top of Jane's arm.

"At the local radio station. She was a kind of runner-cum-admin assistant to the DJs there. She loved her job."

"Have you noticed anyone hanging around the house recently, acting suspicious at all?"

Jane seemed to consider her answer before she replied, "No. I can't think of anything, and Sarah didn't highlight anything of that nature, either. She would have warned me if she'd spotted anyone up to no good, and I would have done the same."

"What about Sarah's next of kin? Do her parents live locally?"

"Oh, Christ! Yes, they live around twenty minutes from here. They'll be devastated. Maybe I should have called them."

"No, that's fine. The news will be better coming from us. It would be good if you had a number for them, though?"

"It's in the house, top drawer in the sideboard in the lounge, in Sarah's address book. She never trusted leaving all her contact numbers in her phone. They all got wiped out a year or so ago, which made her revert back to having a hard-copy type of address book."

"We'll take a look in a moment. Is there anything else you think we should know? I appreciate I'm asking a lot under the circumstances, but anything you can tell us will definitely aid our investigation. How did she get on with her work colleagues, for instance?"

"Okay in the main. I recall she had a problem with one of the DJs, but I think that was sorted pretty quickly."

"Problem? What kind of problem?"

"She briefly told me a DJ had touched her up. She handled it by going to the boss, who sorted it out right away."

"Interesting. When was this?"

"A few months ago now. I think she was still dating Gary back then."

"We'll visit her workplace for the low-down on that, thanks. Anything else you can think of? Did Sarah have other exes, perhaps?"

"No. She was quite fussy whom she dated. Wasn't the type to dump one bloke to start dating another. If anything, I suppose you could say she preferred her freedom to permanently dating someone."

"Thank you. You've been very helpful. Now, we need to get you somewhere to stay for the evening. Maybe a day or two until Forensics have finished their side of things. Do you have anywhere you can go?"

"Yes, I can go back to the hospital, bed down there for the night in one of their emergency dorms on the nurses' wing. Can I grab some things from the flat first?"

"Yes, I'm sure that will be okay once the pathologist gives the all-clear." Kayli handed the young woman a card. "Here's my number. If you think of anything later on you might have missed, please get in touch with me, day or night."

Jane took the card in her shaking hand and tucked it in her coat pocket. "Please, find this disgusting person. Sarah didn't deserve to die. She was so young, had her whole life ahead of her."

"I promise you that we'll certainly do our best. Let me go and have a word with the pathologist. I'll be right back." Kayli and Dave left the car. She turned to Dave and said, "Why don't you sit in your car? I shouldn't be long, then I think we should head back to the station."

"The station? I think we should head over to see the victim's parents first."

Kayli nodded. "You're right. We'll do that. See you in a tick." She stepped into her white paper suit and plastic shoes again and entered the house. "It's only me, Naomi," she shouted as she walked through the front door. At the doorway to the bedroom, she said, "Two things. The witness said the front door was locked when she got home. Can you get your guys to dust it for prints for me? There's also the question of how the assailant exited the building. Maybe he went through the bathroom window, the same way the witness gained access to the property. She's saying the muddy footprint belongs to her."

"Brilliant. Okay, I'll get the team on that in a second or two."

"Last thing. The flatmate is going to have to move out for a day or two, and she needs to pack a bag. All right if she does that?"

"Would you mind accompanying her? We're a little tied up to babysit someone at present."

"Of course. Can I grab a spare suit from your van?"

"Yep, feel free."

Kayli retrieved the paper suit from Naomi's van and gave it to Jane, along with a set of plastic shoes. After donning the suit, Jane hesitantly ascended the steps up to the house. She paused in the doorway to inhale and exhale a few deep breaths before stepping over the threshold.

Kayli smiled at her. "You'll be fine. We'll just throw a few things in a bag and be out in no time at all."

"Thank you. Not sure I could face seeing Sarah again."

"You won't have to. Okay, are you ready?"

"Yes, I think so," she replied, her breath shuddering a little.

Jane pointed out which room was hers, and they both entered the medium-sized room, which had a window facing the front of the property. There were no curtains at the window, only a roller-blind—practical, but less homely. An old white discoloured wardrobe stood in the alcove, and mismatched bedside tables sat on either side of the double bed. Jane pulled down a travel bag from the top of the wardrobe and opened the door. She bundled a few trousers and jumpers into the bag then crossed the room to one of the bedside tables and extracted a handful of underwear. "I need to go in the bathroom to pick up my toothbrush and paste, plus my shampoo and deodorant."

"That's fine. I'll come with you. What about a towel? You'll need one of those too, right?"

"You're right. Thank you. I'm not thinking straight."

Once they were finished, Kayli popped her head into Sarah's bedroom, said farewell to Naomi then escorted Jane off the premises. "Do you have a car?"

"No. I'll get a taxi."

"I'll drop you off. Slip out of your suit and jump in my car."

Jane handed the suit to Kayli, who threw it together with hers into the boot of her car. "I'm going to drop Jane off at the hospital," she called out to Dave. "Will you follow me?"

"Yep. Want me to chase up Donna?"

"Please. I forgot to pick up the address book from the premises. Thinking about it, I better shoot back in and do that now. Sorry, Jane, bear with me a second." Kayli chastised herself for not having all her concentration on the job. She donned the suit again and rushed back inside the house to retrieve the small address book from the top drawer of the sideboard in the lounge. She placed it in an evidence bag and left the house yet again. *Get your act together, girly.*

Kayli had been unusually distracted. With Mark miles away from her and in the hands of the heinous Taliban, it was only natural for her mind to be elsewhere. *Isn't it...? No, I need to concentrate on the murder case in hand. Mark's dilemma will sort itself out in good time, I hope.*

CHAPTER TWO

Dave drew up alongside Kayli's car at the hospital after she dropped Jane off. "Donna's got the address of the parents. Want to head over there now?"

"Yep. That's great. I just flipped through the address book and only found their phone number under 'Mum and Dad'. I'd rather go over and break the news in person. How are you feeling? Your leg, I mean?"

"Stop worrying about me. It's fine while I'm sitting down. I'm thankful the car is an automatic."

She smiled. "I bet you are. Follow me then."

They set off, and ten minutes later, they pulled up outside a detached house situated in a small crescent on the outskirts of the city. Several rooms at the front of the house were lit up.

"Want me to do this alone?" Kayli suggested.

"No, I'd like to be there to show my support and respect to the parents."

"You're one in a million, Dave. Need a hand?"

"Nope, I've got this. It's a well-oiled routine getting out of the car with the aid of these bad boys now."

Within seconds, Dave had manoeuvred capably out of the car and was standing alongside her. Kayli shut the car door for him, and together, they approached the house.

A man in his early sixties, wearing a tartan waistcoat, opened the door. "Hello, can I help you?"

Kayli showed the man her ID. "Hello, Mr. Abel. I'm DI Kayli Bright, and this is my partner, DS Dave Chaplin. We're with the Avon and Somerset Constabulary. Is it possible for us to come in for a moment to have a chat with you and Mrs. Abel?"

"About what?" he asked, frowning.

"Please, sir. We'd rather do this inside."

Hidden Agenda

He stood aside to let them enter the large spacious hallway, which was decorated in a rich burgundy. The staircase was the dominant feature of the room, but there was also a small bookcase along one of the walls, clear of all other clutter, unlike other residencies she'd visited recently.

"What's this about, Inspector? My wife and I are eating dinner."

"I'm sorry to interrupt you."

A door opened behind Mr. Abel, and a woman with beautifully coiffured grey hair entered the hallway. "Frank, what's going on?"

"I've yet to find out, dear. The inspector here was just about to tell me."

"Hello, Mrs. Abel. I'm sorry to disturb your evening. We've just come from your daughter's address. An incident took place there this evening."

"What sort of incident? Strange that Sarah hasn't rung us to let us know," Mr. Abel said.

His wife took a step forward, her gaze locked with Kayli's. "Something has happened to Sarah, hasn't it?" She grasped her husband's arm for support.

Kayli exhaled loudly. "I'm sorry, but your daughter passed away at the scene."

"Passed away? You're not making any sense. You mean she's dead?" Mr. Abel asked, stunned.

Kayli nodded. "Yes. Someone gained access to her house this evening and killed her."

"What? Who? Have you caught this sick individual?"

"No, not yet. We're going to start the investigation as soon as we leave here. We thought you would want to know the news as soon as possible."

"I have to sit down. My legs are shaking," Mrs. Abel said.

Her husband hooked an arm under her elbow and guided her back into the room she'd just left. Mr. Abel ordered offhandedly, "Come through."

Kayli turned to Dave and grimaced. He rolled his eyes up to the ceiling before they followed the couple into the room.

Mr. Abel placed his wife in the armchair close to the bay window and settled himself on the arm alongside her. They clutched hands, and both stared at Kayli.

"Sit down, please," Mrs. Abel requested, her voice wavering a little.

Kayli and Dave sat on the couch opposite them. "I'm sorry to have to break this shocking news to you. I wanted to do it before you saw the story on the TV. There were several TV cameras outside your daughter's house when we left... it doesn't take them long to get wind of things."

"We appreciate that. Please, tell us what happened?" Mr. Abel said.

"It would appear that someone broke into your daughter's flat not long after she arrived home from work."

"Was she... assaulted?" Mrs. Abel asked.

"We don't believe so. She was bound, and... the killer suffocated her with a plastic bag."

Mrs. Abel broke down. Her husband threw an arm around her shoulders. Neither of them spoke again for a few minutes, until Mrs. Abel's sobbing subsided a little.

"What is the motive behind the attack, Inspector, if it wasn't sexual?"

"We've yet to determine that, sir. Her flatmate discovered Sarah's body and called nine-nine-nine straight away."

"So Jane is okay?" Mrs. Abel asked.

"Yes. She's very shaken up, as you can imagine. We dropped her off at the hospital, where she's staying at the nurses' wing, as the pathologist and forensics team are going over the flat with a fine-tooth comb. She'll be allowed to return to the flat after the scene has been processed."

"Did she say if she saw anyone at the flat? Does she know who did this?" Mr. Abel asked.

"No. We asked if either she or Sarah had received any unwanted advances from any men lately, or if they'd noticed anyone watching the flat, but she couldn't think of anything. She was in shock, though, and I've left my card with her. I'm sure she'll be in touch if anything comes to mind."

"What about Gary?" Mrs. Abel suggested.

"The ex-boyfriend?" Kayli replied. "Is there a particular reason you suggested his name?"

"Isn't that the done thing? To question all those people involved with the victim?" Mr. Abel said, finishing off his wife's train of thought.

"Jane told me he's in the navy. I'll be contacting him soon, I can assure you. Can you suggest any other people you think we should be chasing up?" She kept a lid on what Jane had told her about Gary striking Sarah, in case the parents weren't aware of the incident.

"I can't think of any. Frank, can you?" Mrs. Abel asked.

Her husband shook his head as the colour started to drain from each of their faces.

"Did she mention her job at all? What her colleagues were like?" Kayli asked.

"Not really. She always said how well she got on with all of them." Mr. Abel tilted his head. "Are you concerned about something, Inspector?"

Kayli got the impression that he was something to do with the law, a solicitor maybe by the probing questions he was asking. "Jane mentioned an incident with one of the DJs that has piqued my interest. I'll be dropping by to have a word with her colleagues first thing in the morning." She cringed. Maybe she should have kept that snippet to herself as well, judging by the expression on Mr. Abel's face.

"Incident? What type of incident?" Mr. Abel pressed.

"A slight incident. Nothing for you to be concerned about at this stage, Mr. Abel."

He shook his head and snorted. "'Nothing to be concerned about,' you say, and yet our daughter is on her way to the mortuary."

Kayli held his gaze. "At the moment, that's all I can say on the matter until I interview the person involved. It wouldn't be right for me to speak about matters that are pure hearsay. I'm sure we'll get to the bottom of the incident soon enough, sir."

"Have there been any other incidences like this in Sarah's area? Have you looked into that yet, Inspector?"

Mrs. Abel looked up at her husband. "Now, Frank, give the young lady a chance. You know how these things work."

Kayli's brow furrowed. "You do, Mr. Abel?"

"Yes, I'm a solicitor. I'm sorry for asking obvious questions. I realise you've only just come from my daughter's home. Forgive me."

"Nothing to forgive, I assure you. Once we leave here, my team and I won't stop until we have the culprit behind bars. I've already recalled my team to the station after a long day's shift so we can get started immediately."

"That's good to hear, Inspector. Now, if it's all the same to you, we'd like you to leave so that we can grieve our daughter's death in private." Mr. Abel stood up and walked towards the door.

Kayli rose from her seat and shook Mrs. Abel's hand while Dave struggled to get up from the low sofa. "I'm sorry again for your loss. I'll keep you updated with how the investigation is progressing, as and when I can."

Fresh tears filled Mrs. Abel's eyes. "Thank you, Inspector. Please do that."

They joined Mr. Abel at the front door. Kayli extended her hand for him to shake.

He held on to it. "Please do your best for us, Inspector. Don't hesitate to get in touch if you have any questions you require answering."

"Thank you, sir. I'll be in touch soon. Sorry for your loss." Kayli let Dave leave the house before her. She opened the car door for her partner and winced as she watched him struggle to get behind the steering wheel. "I knew he was either a solicitor or someone to do with the law. Let's hope he refrains from interfering with the case. I think this is going to be a tough one, Dave."

"I'm getting the same impression. All we can do is do our best, boss. If he starts putting pressure on us to perform, it could hamper our chances of finding the git who did this."

"I'll make the DCI aware of his involvement in the case first thing. I need a coffee—let's get back to the station."

"All right if I pick up a pizza on the way back? I'm starving."

"Good idea. I could do with a nibble too, if only to keep my energy up."

"Looks like you're still losing weight to me," Dave mumbled.

"Don't start, big man. I have good reason to be off my food. Did you have to bring that up?"

Dave shrugged. "Sorry, just stating the obvious."

CHAPTER THREE

Kayli was surprised, but grateful, to see Graeme sitting at his desk when she marched into the incident room, carrying two pizzas. "Gosh, I must have had a premonition you'd be here. Dave's hobbling up the stairs, so he shouldn't be long. Do you both want a coffee?"

"Yes, please, boss. Donna rang me. I was at the gym with my mate, dropped that, and came straight in," Graeme replied. "I'll get the coffees," he added, jumping out of his seat before she could refuse.

Kayli winked at Donna. "You're a treasure. Thanks for ringing him."

"No problem. It would be strange starting the investigation without him on board. I took the liberty of looking up the victim's Facebook page, boss."

Kayli perched on the desk beside her. "And? Find anything interesting?"

"The usual. I didn't find any form of malicious comments. I went back a couple of months on her wall. That's not to say she hasn't received an unwanted personal message. However, obviously, I can't access that sensitive information without her password."

"Okay, that narrows it down a little anyway. Good thinking, Donna. She has an ex-boyfriend whom we should count as a person of interest. Gary Young. He's in the navy, based in Plymouth. After we've eaten, can you look into that for me? See if he's still on the base down there? He came home on leave a few weeks ago. I can't see him coming home so soon, but it's worth a shot, even to omit him from our enquiries."

Dave barged through the doors and hobbled towards his seat, panting a little. "That's the worst part of having these damn things, walking up the bloody stairs." He collapsed into his chair.

Graeme handed the drinks around while Kayli tore apart the pizza. "Dig in, guys."

Dave took one look at the pizza and screwed up his nose. "Hawaiian, looks the colour of…"

"Don't you dare say it. You'll put everyone off—in fact, you've already done it to me," she said, cottoning on to his suggestion that it was the same colour as the vomit they had witnessed at the victim's address.

"What's this?" Graeme enquired.

"We're not going there. Just enjoy the pizza." She nibbled at the edge of a triangle, trying to block out the image of the victim at the scene. She managed to eat half a slice before her stomach registered it was full.

"That's barely enough to keep a field mouse going… no wonder you're losing weight," Dave said through a mouthful of dough.

"Like I said, you've put me off. Don't let me stop you from eating yours. I'm going to start marking up the board with the details we have so far."

She left her seat, taking her coffee with her, and leaving the other three to munch on their pizza. At the top of the board, she wrote the victim's name and noted down her boyfriend's name. Alongside that, she added the victim's place of work and the fact that she'd had a recent tussle with one of the DJs there. She also noted down Jane Gaunt, the flatmate's name, just for reference. Moments later, Donna joined her at the board.

"I've left them to it, boss. There's only so much pizza a girl can shove down her neck, right? I'm going to try and track down the ex now. Anything specific you want me to ask?"

Kayli smiled at the constable. "The usual, Donna. See if he has any kind of record at the base, that type of thing. They might not tell you, but it's worth a try. The main thing is we find out where he is right now."

"I'm on it." Donna swiftly zigzagged her way through Dave's and Graeme's chairs and desks, back to her seat.

"Come on, guys, how long does it take to eat a couple of pizzas?" Kayli shouted impatiently.

"Usually not long, when people do their bit and share the damn thing with you," Dave yelled back, wiping grease from his chin.

"Graeme, I'd like you to get hold of any CCTV footage in the area. There must be something."

"Yes, boss."

"I also need you to look at CCTV footage around her place of work, the radio station. Maybe someone picked her up from work and gave her a lift home."

Graeme nodded.

"Anything specific you want me to look into, boss?" Dave asked.

"We need to get hold of her phone and financial records, Dave. Plus, I want to start checking into her colleagues' backgrounds. Not liking what I'm hearing on that side of things, either."

"Okey-dokey."

"I'll be in my office if anyone wants me." Carrying her cup, she entered her office and closed the door behind her. She breathed out a heavy sigh and stopped to look out the window at the Bristol city centre skyline, lit up like Blackpool Illuminations. Her gaze rose to the twinkling stars in the dark sky above, as her thoughts travelled the continents to where Mark was being held against his will.

Shaking her head in despair, she sat behind her cluttered desk and extracted her mobile from her jacket pocket. She punched in the number two and waited for her call to connect. "Hey, Giles, it's me."

"Hi, sis. I was going to ring you in a while."

She sat forward in her chair, excited by his words. "You were? Have you heard anything?"

"Sorry to mislead you. No, not heard a dickie bird. Keep your chin up, love. I'm sure we'll hear something positive from the guys over there soon."

She slumped back in her chair again and shook her head as tears formed in her tired eyes. "Really? You think? It's been a couple of weeks, and we haven't heard anything positive so far, Giles. I'm struggling here. Losing my grip on reality at times."

"Don't let it affect your job, love. You're too good for that."

"Easier said than done. Are you telling me that Mark isn't in your thoughts twenty-four-seven? I'd feel heartless if I blocked him out."

"I know it's difficult, Kayli. You just have to dig deep."

"I'm trying. It doesn't help that I have a new case to deal with—a nasty one, at that. I'm in my office now, hiding while my team do all the necessary digging to get the case underway. That's not the way I like to do things, Giles. I've already made a few mistakes on the case this evening. It's a good job I have an excellent partner who turned up at the crime scene. He dug me out of a hole."

"Sorry to hear that, love. Maybe it would be better to put in a request for time off, if that's how this is affecting you."

"And do what? Sit at home, staring at the four walls and hope these evil monsters will eventually free him?"

Giles remained silent, and Kayli suspected that was because he had no further wise words on the subject. "What's taking your guys so long to find out where he is?"

"Crikey, Kayli. They're doing their best. It's a vast country, and they could be holding him anywhere. The intel is that the Taliban prefer to hide out in caves. The terrain is riddled with them. It's not like you tracking down a suspect in this country with the aid of CCTV. This is still regarded as a primitive country, once you get away from the major towns."

"I know. It's just all so frustrating. Makes me wonder if I would do better over there."

Giles laughed. "You might think that from the safety of your office, but being stuck out there in the middle of nowhere, amidst sandstorms and under enemy fire, would soon change your mind, I can assure you."

Kayli picked up a pen and threw it across her desk. "I know you're right." She sighed heavily as her words dried up.

"Stay strong, girl. Why don't you come round for dinner tomorrow? Annabelle and Bobby would love to see you."

"Hmm... not so sure about that. I'm as miserable as sin at present. I'd hate to take my foul mood out on either of them. Plus, there's no telling what hours I'll be putting in over the next few days not with a killer on the loose."

"Okay, I hear you. The offer still stands, though."

"Thanks, Giles. Give Anabelle and Bobby a hug from me. I hope the morning sickness has subsided for Annabelle."

"She says it's bearable. She still has to watch what she eats regarding any greasy meals. I'll give them a hug. Sis, take care of yourself. Have faith in our guys rescuing Mark, all right?"

"I'll try. I better go now. Love to all."

She ended the call, and hearing a knock on her door, she called out, "Come in."

Donna poked her head around the door, her eyes sparkling with what looked like excitement. "Good news, boss, well, sort of."

"Hit me with it, Donna. I could definitely use some of that right now."

"I managed to speak to Gary Young's commanding officer. He told me that Gary had been given compassionate leave on the grounds of his mother dying of cancer."

"And that's good news?" Kayli replied, miffed by the constable's logic.

"Sorry, yes, in a roundabout way, boss. His mother lives in Bristol, so that would place him in this area, not in Plymouth."

Kayli nodded firmly. "Now you're making sense. We need to trace his vehicle ASAP and his address and that of his mother, or is she in hospital due to her illness?"

"I asked the commanding officer, and he wasn't sure where the mother is, but he gave me the address that Gary calls home when he's on leave. He believes it's his mother's address."

"Good, we need to get someone round there. See if uniform can do a drive-by for us to make sure the car is there first."

Donna nodded. "I'll ring them right away."

"Before you go, Donna, has Graeme managed to locate the CCTV footage yet?"

"Yes, it's just come through."

"Okay. I'll be out in a few minutes." Kayli finished the rest of her lukewarm coffee and followed Donna out of the office. Her stomach churned, as it always did when she felt a suspect was in her grasp.

They waited patiently for the call to come in from the officers on the street. When it did, the news wasn't good. There was no sign of Young's car at his mother's address. Kayli was tempted to go round there, but her conscience warned her not to cause a dying woman extra stress. They had no firm evidence yet that Young was the perpetrator. Just because he was in Bristol at the time of his ex-girlfriend's death meant nothing.

"Come on, guys. We need something. Dave, anything on either the phone or the financials yet?"

Dave shook his head. "Nothing showing up on either that could be deemed as suspicious."

Kayli punched her thigh. "Damn. It's down to you to find something on the footage then. Graeme, anything so far?"

"Nothing near her flat. I'm widening the search to the adjoining main roads, boss. I'm sure that if anything is there, I'll find it soon."

Kayli glanced up at the clock on the wall. At just past eight o'clock, the golden hour had passed, and they were nowhere near solving the heinous crime.

Another hour dragged by before Graeme shouted for Kayli to look at something on his screen. She rushed over to his desk and leaned close to the image. "That's the victim. She's getting into a vehicle. We need to get a registration on that car if we can, Graeme."

"Leave it with me, boss."

"Do we know what car Young drives?"

"A blue Ford Focus, boss," Donna called back.

Kayli shook her head and looked at Graeme. "That isn't a Focus, is it?"

"No, boss. Looks like a Beemer to me."

"Yep, I was thinking along those lines too. It's imperative we get a registration on that car, Graeme." She watched him manipulate the image without success. "Wait, what's that?" Kayli pointed to the bottom of the screen. "Can you zoom in on that? It looks like a reflection of the car in the shop window opposite."

"I think I can. Bear with me a second."

He tinkered with the keys until the plate came into focus.

"That's it. Well done, Graeme. Get me a name for that driver."

Within minutes, they had located the name and address of the driver.

"Donna, can you try and track down a number for me? Wait, never mind. Dave, we need to visit the driver ASAP."

Dave shrugged. "Fine by me. All right if you drive? My leg's a bit sore."

Guilt wrapped around her shoulders. "Damn, sorry, matey. Why don't you go home? We can handle things around here."

"Why? I've never run out on you before when you needed me, and I'm not about to start now. I'll be fine. I'll pop a couple of painkillers before we leave."

Kayli crossed the room to fetch him a cup of water and waited for him to swallow the tablets. "Ready?"

He chased the pills with another sip of water. "As I'll ever be."

"Right, Mr. Danny Talbot, let's see what you have to say for yourself? Graeme, while we're gone, keep trying to locate Young's vehicle."

Graeme raised his thumb in the air in confirmation.

CHAPTER FOUR

Kayli exited the car at the address in Clifton that Donna had supplied them with. Waiting for Dave to get out of the car, she surveyed the neighbourhood around the terraced house. This road had always suffered from a bad reputation, until the regeneration project had started a few months ago. Now that the council had shipped out the riffraff they had identified as the biggest trouble-makers, the residents seemed to be taking more pride in their homes, judging by the cut hedges and the number of hanging baskets on show. Once Dave was ready, she walked up the short path and rang the bell.

"How's the leg now?" she asked as they waited for the door to be answered.

Dave tilted his head from side to side. "So-so. It'll be fine soon. I'll plod on regardless."

"You're a good man, Dave."

A good-looking man in his thirties opened the door. He wore a thick grey jumper and jeans. "Hello? Can I help?"

"Are you Danny Talbot?"

He frowned. "That's right. Look, if this is some kind of survey, I'm not interested."

"It's not." Kayli produced her ID. "DI Kayli Bright, and this is my partner, DS Dave Chaplin. All right if we come in for a chat?"

"About what, may I ask?"

Kayli smiled. "Inside would be better, sir."

He stood behind the door and motioned for them to enter the hallway, the frown never shifting from his face. "First door on the right is the lounge. Excuse the mess, I've not long got in from work."

Kayli and Dave followed his directions and walked into the room, where an empty fish and chip carton lay on the coffee table.

"Please take a seat. May I ask what this is about, Inspector?" He sat down on the sofa closest to the TV and invited Dave and Kayli to sit opposite him on a two-seater leather sofa in a contrasting colour.

"We're investigating a crime that took place this evening, sir. During our investigation, your vehicle was highlighted at the scene. We'd like to ask you some questions about the incident, if that's okay?"

"I'm confused. Are you saying that you think my vehicle was used in a crime? I can assure you the car hasn't been out of my possession today, and I have no knowledge of me being involved in any car crime," he replied defensively.

Kayli exhaled a breath. "I'm sorry. It's been a very long day. Maybe I didn't make myself clear enough. Do you know a Sarah Abel?"

His frown deepened. "Of course I know her. She's a work colleague of mine."

"Thank you. May I ask why she was seen getting into your vehicle at approximately five fifteen this evening?"

He shrugged and held his hands up in front of him. "Because I was giving her a lift home from work. Her car is in the workshop. What are you insinuating here, Inspector?"

Kayli's lips parted slightly. "What time did you drop her off, sir?"

He paused to think for a second. "Gosh, hang on. I think it was around five thirty. Why? What has she said?" he asked, his voice rising a few octaves.

"She hasn't said anything, Mr. Talbot, because Miss Abel was found dead earlier this evening."

He jumped out of his chair, his hand running through his hair in frantic strokes. "She what? I don't believe it. Dead? How? Was she killed in some kind of accident?"

"Please take a seat, sir. No, unfortunately she was murdered in her flat. Her flatmate found her less than an hour after you dropped her off."

He fell onto the sofa again, looking shocked. "My God! I can't quite believe what I'm hearing. Who would do such a thing? Was it a burglary? Was there an intruder in her house when I dropped her off? Crap! I should have walked her to her door at least."

"We're not really sure what happened yet, as we're still trying to piece things together. During the journey, how was Sarah?"

"How was she? I don't understand what you're getting at? She was alive!"

"Sorry, let me try that again. Was Sarah apprehensive at all?"

He shook his head. "No. We chatted, like we always do."

"Is it a regular occurrence for you to give her a lift home?"

"Not really. I overheard her telling one of our colleagues that her car was in the workshop for repairs. I volunteered to give her a lift home as we usually leave around the same time." His head dropped onto his chest. "Why didn't I go into the flat with her?"

"Hindsight is a wonderful thing in cases such as this. Please, there's no point blaming yourself. Did you see anyone near her flat when she left your vehicle?"

He looked up and met her gaze. "There were a few people leaving their cars, coming home from work—a typical suburban setting, I suppose you could say. No one that struck me as being a killer." The final word, he said quieter than the rest of his statement.

"Did you watch Sarah enter her flat, or did you drive away before she reached her front door?"

"No, I drove off as soon as she left my car. Had I known she was in danger, I would have stuck around, obviously."

Kayli smiled. "You mustn't blame yourself."

"That's going to be mighty hard, Inspector. I was probably the last person to ever see her alive... that's tough to take."

"I can understand that. We need to try and find a motive for someone killing her. Do you have any ideas? During your chats, did she hint at anyone she was concerned about?"

He remained silent for a few moments as he mulled over her question. "I know she split up with her boyfriend a few months back. Of course, I'm not aware of the ins and outs of the break-up."

"Have you ever met the ex-boyfriend, Gary Young? Perhaps at a work's function?"

"No, I don't believe I have."

"What about at work? Was everything okay on that front for Sarah?"

"As far as I know. No one at work would be capable of killing her."

"That statement can be attributed to a lot of killers, sir. Unfortunately, murderers don't have the word tattooed across their forehead. The fact is, something triggers the anger gene in most of them, turning them into killers."

"I'm at a loss what to say to that, Inspector. I don't profess to know what goes on in the mind of a killer." He shuddered at the thought.

"Okay. If there's nothing else you can add to our enquiry, we better get on with our investigation. Thank you for speaking to us. My condolences."

"Good luck with your investigation," he said, standing up.

He showed Kayli and Dave to the front door. She handed him a business card, which he tucked into the pocket of his jeans. Then he shook her hand. Kayli noticed his hand was clammy, pointing to how much the news must have shocked him.

They were settled back in the car, en route to the station, before Dave spoke. "Poor sod is riddled with guilt."

Kayli sighed. "I think I would be too, if I had given Sarah a lift home and she'd wound up dead less than an hour later."

"I suppose. It's looking more and more like the boyfriend, right?"

"It is, but I'd rather have some evidence to back up that suspicion. At the moment, all we have is that Young is in the area."

"Why don't we pay him a visit? Ruffle his feathers a little."

Kayli stared at the brake lights of the car in front of her as they came to a standstill at the traffic lights. "Ring Donna for me. See if uniform have located Young's car at his mother's address."

Dave rang the station and put the phone on speaker. "Donna, it's Dave. Any news on Young?"

"Uniform just got back to me to say that his car drew up at the address a few minutes ago as they were leaving."

"Good news. Donna, we're going over there to speak to him. Has Graeme managed to pick Young's car up on the footage?"

"He's managed to place him a couple of roads from the victim's flat at around the time she got home from work."

"Brilliant. Can you tell the patrol car to turn around and meet us at the address? We might need some backup, what with Dave hobbling around on crutches at the mo," Kayli asked.

"I'll do it now, boss."

"Give me the address again, if you would?"

"Seventeen Forsythia Drive, boss,"

"Thanks, Donna." Dave ended the call.

"I know the road. My friend used to live there. We should be there in under ten minutes. You stay in the car, let me and the uniformed lads deal with the situation. Got that?"

Dave tutted. "Damn leg. I would have revelled in the chance to give him a good slapping for resisting arrest, if it comes to that."

Kayli laughed. "Good job you're incapacitated in that case."

CHAPTER FIVE

Kayli's heart was beating faster than normal when she knocked on the front door of the mid-terraced house. Two thick-set uniformed officers stood alongside her as they waited for the door to open. "Let me do the talking before you guys pounce."

The officers nodded. Kayli saw a light go on in the hallway through the paned glass at the top of the door. A clean-shaven young man wearing jeans and a T-shirt opened the door.

"What's all this?" he asked, staring at them.

"Gary Young?" Kayli asked in an authoritative tone.

"That's right. What's going on?" He eased the door shut a little.

"We'd like you to accompany us to the station for questioning."

"Who is it, dear?" a frail voice called out from a room off the hallway.

"It's all right, Mum... it's the police. I won't be long. Stay in the lounge, where it's warm."

Kayli couldn't tell if his compassion was genuine or whether it was all an act for their benefit.

He shook his head in disbelief. "Have I done something wrong?"

"Sarah Abel was found murdered in her flat earlier this evening. Do you need to call someone to look after your mother? She has cancer, doesn't she?"

He stumbled backwards, clutching a hand to his chest. "What? Sarah is dead? I don't believe it... Damn, and you think I have something to do with it? Are you *crazy*?"

"Yes. Can you answer my question about your mother?"

"I can get my neighbour to sit with her while I help you with your *enquiries*," he replied sarcastically.

"Do that. You have five minutes," Kayli told him sharply.

Kayli raised her eyebrows, gesturing for one of the officers to accompany Young, just in case he decided to make a run for it.

Hidden Agenda

He brushed past them and walked across the small front lawn to knock on his neighbour's door, with the officer close on his tail.

A few minutes later, a woman with grey hair and wearing slippers, followed Young back across the garden and into the house.

Gary glared at Kayli. "Stay here. I don't want my mother upset any more than is necessary. I'll just get my coat and put on some shoes."

Kayli nodded and waited for Young to reappear. She heard his mother asking questions through her sobs. Kayli's heart went out to the woman, but she had a job to do, and at the moment, Gary Young was their prime suspect.

Young reappeared, shrugging on a denim jacket. "Okay. Do you want to slap on the handcuffs, or are you going to trust me? Seeing that I've done nothing wrong."

"As a precaution, we're going to handcuff you." Kayli read him his rights as his mouth dropped open.

"You said you were taking me in for questioning, and now you're arresting me? For Sarah's murder? But I haven't seen her in weeks."

"Yes. We'll discuss the complexities of the situation back at the station. Are you ready?" She extracted a roll of plastic food bags from her pocket, tore off two of the bags, and placed one on each of his hands before one of the officers slapped the cuffs on him.

"No, but that's not going to stop you from hauling me in. Can I just say that you're making a huge mistake, and if Sarah has been murdered, you're allowing the real killer to get away? I'm innocent, Inspector—I promise you that."

"We'll see. Do you want to ring your solicitor, or shall we appoint a duty solicitor for you?"

"I want my solicitor by my side if you're going to fit me up with something I haven't done."

"You can place the call when we get to the station."

The officers escorted Young from the garden and placed him in the back of their car.

"See you back at the station, guys," Kayli said, getting in her own vehicle.

"Well, looks like he's none too happy," Dave noted.

"He's denying it. I have to admit, his reaction was quite disconcerting."

"Now don't go getting soft on me. Once you present the evidence of his car being in the vicinity of her address around the time of her murder, you watch, I bet his attitude changes pretty damn quick."

"We'll see. He's put in a request for his own solicitor to attend the interview. So any questions I have to ask will have to be delayed. You know how these solicitors like to drag their feet."

"Well, he better get a wriggle on. We can only hold him for twenty-four hours."

"Umm... yes, I'm aware of that snippet of information, thanks Dave."

He gave her a cheesy grin. "Sorry."

She treated him to a grin of her own before she punched his arm. Kayli followed the patrol car back to the station. Upon their arrival, Young was allowed to call his solicitor, then Kayli asked the desk sergeant to place Young in a cell until his solicitor showed up. "Can you get Mr. Young's DNA before he enters his cell and issue a change of clothes? Forensics will need to go over them thoroughly. Thanks, Sergeant."

Dave was halfway up the stairs before she caught up with him. "Need a hand?"

"Nope. I'll take it steady. I'll need a cup of coffee when I make it to the top, though."

Kayli ran on ahead, shouting over her shoulder, "Your wish is my command."

Her adrenaline was kicking in now that there was a suspect sitting in a cell. It was up to her and her team to gather all they had on Young to ensure the charges stuck.

"He's downstairs in a cell, guys," she announced as she breezed into the incident room.

"Brilliant news, boss. I'm still tracking his vehicle through the city on the ANPR cameras," Graeme told her, a large smile stretching his mouth.

"Coffee all round then, guys. Let's do our best to get our victim the justice she deserves. I need to action a warrant for his mother's house. Can you organise that for me, Donna?"

Donna picked up the phone and punched in a few numbers. "On it, now, boss."

Kayli sorted through her purse for some change then inserted the coins in the machine. Dave hobbled into the incident room, his face red from his exertions, and fell into his chair as she deposited his coffee on his desk. "Are you sure you don't want to go home? We've got the suspect now. There's no point in you hanging around, matey."

"Now you tell me? You could've mentioned that while we were downstairs in the damn car park," Dave replied, his eyes narrowing.

Kayli cringed. "Sorry, I never thought."

"It's a good job I'm only winding you up then. I'm fine. You worry too much. I'm here for the duration—we all are. Right, team?"

Donna and Graeme both nodded. "I'm blessed to have you guys around me. I really appreciate you all going the extra mile on this one. Looks like our endeavours have paid off too."

~ ~ ~

Less than thirty minutes later, the desk sergeant called to tell Kayli that Young's solicitor was waiting at the front desk. She looked at her watch—it was almost ten o'clock. "Wow, that's gotta be some kind of record. Mind you, he'll probably screw his client and bill him for double time." She laughed and walked towards the door.

"Hey, you're not going to question him alone, are you?" Dave shouted.

"Damn! No, I better not do that. Donna, fancy joining me?"

"Wow, yes. That would be great. Do I need to bring anything?"

"Your notebook and pen will suffice," Kayli replied, amused by the young constable's enthusiasm, even if it was this deep into her shift. As they walked down the stairs together, Kayli could hear Donna's heavy breathing. "Hey, you need to calm down a bit, Donna. You'll be no good to me if you're full of anxiety."

Donna sucked in a large breath and let it out slowly. "I'm good, boss."

They halted at the bottom of the stairs. "Okay, wait here. I'll collect the solicitor and see what interview room is available."

She walked into the reception area to find a tall, slim, bespectacled blonde woman holding a briefcase. "Hello, I'm DI Kayli Bright."

The solicitor shook her hand. "Gemma Jordache, pleased to meet you."

"Which room shall we use, Sergeant?"

"Room Two is set up for you, ma'am. I'll get a PC to bring the suspect through in a moment."

"Shall we?" Kayli said to the solicitor then nodded for Donna to join them.

The three of them walked down the hallway into Interview Room Two, and Gary Young joined them not long after. His red-rimmed eyes were evidence that he'd been crying in his cell. *Is that guilt, or is he truly upset by Sarah's death?*

Kayli said the necessary verbiage for the tape and introduced everyone in the room. "Right, Mr. Young, or is it all right if I call you Gary?"

"Do what you like. For the tape, I'd just like to say that you've made a huge mistake and that I'm innocent." He turned to Gemma Jordache. "I swear, it wasn't me."

"Just answer the inspector's questions honestly for now, Gary."

"I will. Don't worry. I have nothing to hide."

"You're based in Plymouth, at the naval base. Is that right?"

"Yes."

"How often do you come home on leave?" Kayli asked.

"Quite regularly, due to Mum's health."

Kayli nodded. "I see. And is that why you've come home this weekend?"

"Yes. I'm here for an extra day as Mum has a consultant's appointment at the hospital on Monday, and I told her that I'd go with her."

"Was it your intention to visit Sarah Abel's flat this evening? Or did you happen to drop by on the off-chance?"

"I didn't see Sarah this evening. And if anyone has suggested I did, they're lying. I can't believe she's dead." He ran his hands through his hair.

"Perhaps you can explain why your car was seen within a few metres of Sarah's flat then?"

His gaze dropped to the table, and he stared at his hands twisting together. "No, I can't."

"But you adamantly denied going near her flat when I questioned you at your mother's house. Why was that?"

He shrugged.

"Can you understand why I arrested you?"

"No. I think you're clutching at straws. Just because I was in the area, it doesn't mean that I killed her."

"So, why were you in the area? Did you see Sarah tonight?" she pressed, despite Young telling her he hadn't seen the victim.

"I can't deny I was there. I was going to tell her that Mum doesn't have long to live, but decided against it."

"Why? What changed your mind?"

"I just did. Perhaps I thought she might think it was me trying to get a sympathy vote from her to win her back. I don't know. My head is all over the place because of Mum's illness. She's losing weight rapidly, and there's not a damn thing I can do about it."

"Are you saying you pulled up outside her place only to drive off again?"

"Yes."

Kayli tilted her head. "I find that incredibly hard to believe. Why would you come all that way with the intention of seeing her, only to turn away at the last moment?"

"I just did."

"Why?" Kayli slammed her hand on the table.

Gary jumped. His hands twisted until the whites of his knuckles showed. "I just did. Like I said, my head is all over the place at the moment because of what Mum is going through."

"Which could be why you're not thinking straight and likely to do things out of character."

He shook his head. "I'm not stupid. I can see where this is leading. I did *not* kill my ex-girlfriend, Inspector."

"Perhaps you can tell me why you split up in the first place? Was it her decision or yours?"

"I believe it was a joint decision. I'm stationed in Plymouth, and the distance between us was causing friction... well, not exactly friction but..."

"You weren't getting on as well as you had previously. Is that what you're saying?"

"Yes. Only without the inference that you put in that question. Although we split up, we still remained friends—good friends."

"Good friends? And yet you hadn't told her about your mother's illness? Hasn't she been ill for some time?"

He sighed and sat back in his chair, his gaze meeting hers. "Of course she was aware of Mum's illness. I was going to tell her just how bad Mum had got lately. They used to be close, I thought Sarah might want to visit her."

"So, what prevented you from doing that?"

The corner of his eye began to twitch, and he drew his bottom lip into his mouth.

"Gary?" she prompted when he didn't respond.

"I saw her..."

Kayli shuffled forward in her chair. "But you specifically told me that you hadn't seen her tonight."

"I lied. I saw her, but we didn't speak. All right, all right, I went to see her tonight. I parked outside her flat and waited for her to come home. That's when I saw her kissing him."

"Kissing who?"

"I don't know. The guy in the BMW."

"We're aware that a colleague gave her a lift home from work this evening. Are you telling me they kissed when he dropped her off?"

"Yes. That was enough for me. I thought there was no point hanging around if she'd found someone else. So I left."

"Did you really? Well, I think a different scenario played out. I put it to you that you went to see Sarah, maybe saw her giving her colleague a peck to say thank you for going out of his way to give her a lift home, and it riled you. Made you angry to see that she'd moved on with her life since your break-up. You then entered her house and punished her by ending her life."

Young shook his head adamantly. "That really couldn't be further from the truth. We've been in touch via social media for months. If you look back on those messages, you'd see none of them were either vindictive or angry. Check my phone, for fuck's sake, you'll find the same on there too. I loved her. Whether she was with me or not, I only wanted the best for her."

"Oh, don't worry, I'll be digging into your Facebook account and your phone records, I can assure you."

He gave a defeated shrug. "I'll even give you my passwords to prove I have nothing to hide. You have to believe me, Inspector. You're seriously barking up the wrong tree by arresting me. All you're doing is allowing the real perpetrator to get away." His clenched fist hit the desk, making the three women jump. "You have to believe me. Why haven't you processed my DNA yet? I gave that willingly earlier in the hope that it would exonerate me."

"Calm down, Gary. You're not doing yourself any favours. The DNA results should be back in a few hours, if we're lucky. I've asked Forensics to rush the tests through. If, as you say, you are innocent, then you won't mind spending a few hours in a cell until your innocence has been proven."

He shook his head and turned to face his solicitor. "Is she for real? Is that skewed logic or what?"

"My client does have a point, Inspector," Gemma Jordache said, one of her beautifully structured eyebrows rising into her fringe.

"Maybe. We'll soon find out in a few hours. If I'm wrong, then I will apologise."

"Oh, you're wrong all right, and when it comes to light, you're going to do more than apologise. I won't let this drop, Inspector. You have my word on that." Young flung his arms up in the air out of frustration.

"We'll see. If you're willing to help us, then you can supply us with your passwords for your phone and Facebook. That is if you've got nothing to hide."

"My client has already stated that he would have no problem doing just that, Inspector. In return, I think you should let him go home so that he can tend to his sick mother."

"I'd rather check the information out first, Miss Jordache, and suffer Mr. Young's wrath if I'm proved wrong. I have a responsibility to the general public not to let a possible killer loose on a whim. A few more hours in a cell won't hurt him."

Young chewed the inside of his mouth, obviously seething. He held out his hand for Donna to pass him her notebook and pen. Kayli nodded, and Donna handed them over. They watched Young scribble down his passwords.

"Did you use any other social media to contact Sarah? What's App, Instagram, perhaps?"

"No. Believe it or not, the navy keeps me rather busy most of the time. It's not as if I'm unemployed, sitting on my arse, doing bugger all every day."

"It was a simple question. Thank you for your passwords. We'll still need to wait for the DNA results to come back. But thank you for your cooperation. One last question. Have you ever laid a hand on Sarah?"

"Yes, it happened once, and I regretted my actions immediately. You have to believe me."

"Is that the real reason your relationship ended?"

"No." He sighed then added reluctantly, "It might have been."

Kayli ended the interview, then the PC escorted Young back to his cell.

"I think you're wrong about him, Inspector," Gemma Jordache said as soon as her client left the room.

"If I am, then so be it, Miss Jordache. I have to go with the evidence presented to me. The fact that your client initially disputed being anywhere near Sarah Abel's flat this evening, plus that he laid a hand on her during their relationship, should raise suspicion in your mind too."

The pretty solicitor winced. "Maybe you're right. All I'm saying is that I've known Mr. Young and his family for over ten years and have never felt that he has ever lied to me."

"Glad to hear it. But what he's told us in this interview room has just shot that notion down in flames. Liars tend to lie to cover their tracks. We'll continue our investigation until I get to the truth."

Kayli walked to the door. Gemma Jordache shrugged her slim shoulders and strode past her, up the hallway, and through the reception area.

"Good news about the phone and the Facebook account, boss," Donna pointed out as they began their ascent up the stairs.

"That reminds me... you go ahead and get started on the Facebook account, and I'll pick up his mobile from the desk sergeant."

Donna nodded and ran ahead with her notebook in hand. Kayli turned back to the reception area, her mind foggy with information, doubting her own actions about locking Gary Young up again. Once she'd signed out Young's phone, she raced up the stairs as fast as her weary legs would carry her and into the incident room.

After quickly bringing Dave and Graeme up to speed on how the interview had gone, she and Donna checked through the suspect's messages. "Nothing. It's all general chit-chat, nothing to say how he feels about her or any form of regrets from either side. Maybe he's telling the truth after all."

"Bummer," Dave said. "If that's the case, then who killed Sarah Abel? Was it a burglary gone wrong?"

Kayli tutted and sighed heavily. "I really don't know. There's little more we can do now. Why don't we call it a night? Go home, get a few hours of sleep, and attack things in the morning. We should have the DNA results back by then. I really don't want to set him free without having those in my hand."

"Agreed. It won't hurt for him to be locked up in his cell for a few more hours, whether he's innocent or guilty," Dave agreed.

Hidden Agenda

"I want to thank you all for coming back this evening. It was worth a punt, although the odds are against us on this one, I fear. We'll have to see what tomorrow brings."

CHAPTER SIX

It was close to eleven o'clock by the time Kayli inserted her key in the front door. She paused on the doorstep before she placed a foot over the threshold, preparing herself for the overwhelming feeling of loneliness. She knew that sleep would evade her again. No matter how tired she felt, every time she dared to close her eyes, vile images of Mark being tortured were cast across her eyelids. The only nights she'd managed to avoid that were the nights she spent on the sofa. Deciding she needed a good night's rest, she ran upstairs to collect her pillow and duvet from her bed then made up the couch for the night.

Kayli went through to the kitchen to make a coffee. She was still full from the pizza she'd eaten hours before, so she didn't bother to look in the fridge. Instead, she switched on Sky news. The headline strap at the bottom of the screen read: Woman's body found in her flat in the heart of the city.

The speculation coming from the journalist's mouth made her laugh a few times. Her need to track down a suspect quickly had put paid to her usual routine of using the media to spread the word. However, grave doubts as to whether Young was the killer had crept into her mind, and the chances of him being set free in the morning were quite high. She would likely need to look at using the media in the near future. She sighed, not envying herself having to announce to the community that a killer was on the loose in Bristol. There had been enough murders on their streets lately, most of which had fallen into her lap to solve. She was tired of dealing with people's anger issues. *Why can't people learn to live alongside each other harmoniously, like they used to in the olden days? But did they really?* She shuddered at the BBC programme she'd seen recently, which depicted the story of Guy Fawkes and the gunpowder plot. Innocent people, such as priests, had been treated in such appalling, barbaric ways. She shook her head to rid her mind of the grotesque images of people being hung, drawn and quartered, and stretched on racks. The last thing she wanted was to be reminded of what deplorable conditions Mark was in or what degrading torture the Taliban were subjecting him to.

She undressed, ran upstairs to clean her teeth then snuggled down under her duvet. As her eyelids began to droop, she flicked off the TV and let sleep overcome her.

~ ~ ~

Her phone alarm went off at seven the following morning. She couldn't believe that she'd managed to sleep nearly eight hours. Feeling refreshed, she stretched and took her bedding back upstairs before she jumped in the shower.

Kayli arrived at work just after eight o'clock to find Donna already sitting at her computer. She smiled warmly at the constable. "Morning, Donna, have you been here long?"

"About ten minutes, boss."

"Any news on the DNA results?"

"Yes. Nothing matched Young. Looks like he's in the clear."

Kayli thumped her thigh. "Damn, I know we had an inkling that was going to be the case. However, the reality hurts when it hits."

"What's that?" Dave said, barging through the doors on his crutches.

"The DNA is a no-go for Young."

"Shit. Umm... that's nothing compared to what I've just heard downstairs."

Kayli blew out a breath and perched on the desk behind her. "Okay, I know I'm not going to like the sound of this. What have you heard?"

"I was walking through the reception area when I heard the desk sergeant mention the name Young. I stopped to wait and see what the outcome was."

She gestured with her hand for him to hurry up. "Come on, Dave. Get to the point, man."

"Well, apparently it was the hospital ringing to inform us that Mrs. Young took a tumble down the stairs last night. She's in hospital with a broken hip."

"Damn, shit and blast! Oh, fuck! That's all we frigging need," Kayli replied, rubbing the back of her neck.

"Not good news, eh?" Dave replied.

Kayli let out a frustrated breath. "We should have released him last night. The onus lies on my shoulders—no one else's. Got that?"

Dave shook his head. "It's hardly your fault, boss. You were just following procedures," he stated, trying to make her feel better.

"Thanks, Dave, but I know that's bullshit." She looked up at the clock on the wall. At twenty past eight, it would be too soon to catch the DCI. "I'll need to see Davis at nine, make her aware of this before she hears it from someone else. Right... thinking caps on, guys. First of all, I need to sanction Young's release. I'll organise a patrol car to take him to the hospital to be with his mother, to make amends for screwing up. I can see me getting pulled over the coals for this."

"Nonsense. You're overthinking this, boss," Dave said, dropping into his chair.

"I wish I had your faith. I'll be in my office until nine. I'm sure I'll get summoned then anyway." She heaved herself off the desk and walked over to the vending machine. "Anyone else wants to join me in drowning their sorrows in a cup of coffee?"

Both Dave and Donna nodded, no hint of a smile on either of their faces.

"Hey, guys, there's no need for you to feel glum. Your necks will be safe. I can assure you of that."

"Look, if you go down for this, then we go with you, not that I can foresee you getting into bother for carrying out procedures," Dave insisted, placing his hands on his head and leaning back in his chair.

Kayli distributed the coffee and went into her office. She picked up the phone and rang reception. "Ray? It's DI Bright. Dave's just informed me about Young's mother. We better set him free. The DNA results have come back proving his innocence anyway."

"Very well, ma'am. I'll action that request immediately."

"Thanks, Ray. Look, as a goodwill gesture, can you organise a lift to the hospital for him?"

"Of course I can."

"Thanks. If he starts kicking up a fuss, give me a shout, and I'll come down and speak to him."

"I'm sure everything will be fine, ma'am. Leave it with me."

Hidden Agenda

Kayli ended the call and took a long swig of her coffee. Looking at the post that had miraculously appeared overnight on her already-cluttered desk, she groaned. "Why do they heap so much crap on us? How are we supposed to rid the streets of criminals if we have to contend with this dross day in, day out?" Receiving no answer from above, she ripped open the first letter, scanned the contents, sorted it, and moved on to the next.

Five minutes later, her landline rang. "Hello. DI Bright. How can I help?"

"Sorry, ma'am. It's Ray on reception. Would you mind coming down for a moment? Mr. Young is insisting on having a word with you."

Kayli groaned. "I thought he might. I'm on my way."

She pushed back her chair and rushed through the incident room and down the stairs. In reception, she found Young pacing, his face flushed with anger.

"You wanted to see me, Mr. Young?"

He laughed. "You swan in here as if everything is okay. Yes, I demanded to see you. I want to make it perfectly clear why I intend coming after you for inept policing, Inspector. Right from the outset, I categorically told you that I had nothing to do with Sarah's death, but you chose to ignore me. The upshot of that is that you took me away from caring for my dying mother—now look what's happened. She's writhing around in pain in the hospital. She wouldn't have been in this predicament had I been there looking after her. I blame you for the extra suffering she's incurred, and I won't let this rest until you're at least demoted."

"What can I say, except to give you my sincere apologies? I was merely carrying out my job, Mr. Young. Maybe if you hadn't lied about your whereabouts from the beginning, perhaps I would have released you last night, giving you the opportunity to care for your mother. Perhaps you should look closer to home before you start striking out and blaming others, Mr. Young."

"That's bollocks, and you know it! I hope you've got a good solicitor. You're going to need one," he shouted.

Just then, a draught from the front door wafted through the reception area, and in walked DCI Davis. She frowned, eyeing up the situation, before her gaze landed on Kayli. "May I ask what's going on here?"

Young stepped towards the DCI, making her retreat a little. "I'll tell you what's going on. This so-called inspector banged me up in a cell despite me telling her I was innocent of the crime she reckons I committed. During my stay in the cell, my frail, cancer-riddled mother fell down the stairs at home because no one was there to care for her. Who are you?"

The DCI's shoulders arched back. "I'm DCI Davis, Inspector Bright's senior officer."

"Good. I'm glad I have the chance to speak to you. To warn you. There will be a charge of negligence dropping on your desk within the next few days."

"I'll look forward to seeing that, sir. Sorry, who are you?"

Kayli almost sniggered at the DCI's comeback.

"I'm Gary Young. Remember that name. You're going to be hearing a lot of it in the future. I won't let this rest until that bitch is stripped of her rank. You hear me? All of you will rue the day you threw me in a bloody cell."

"I'll be sure to look out for your letter, Mr. Young. I think it's time you left our station now, don't you?"

"I've arranged for a patrol car to take you to the hospital, Mr. Young," Kayli announced with a taut smile.

"You can stick your offer up your arse. I'll hail a taxi instead."

Kayli shrugged. "As you wish. Goodbye, and once again, I'm sorry regarding your mother's accident."

He grunted, barged past the DCI, almost spinning her a hundred and eighty degrees, and stormed out of the building.

"Well, that was a rude start to my morning. I think we should have a chat in my office ASAP, Inspector, don't you?"

Kayli gulped. "I've been waiting for you to arrive, ma'am. I had every intention of bringing you up to date on the case first thing."

"Good. Walk with me."

The silence as they walked up the stairs and along the long corridor to the DCI's office, was the worst form of torture Kayli could think of in the circumstances. The DCI said hello to her secretary, Fiona, before she entered her office. "Take a seat. Do you want a coffee?"

"No, thank you, ma'am. I've just had one," Kayli replied, sinking into the chair in front of the DCI's desk.

DCI Davis spent the next few minutes ignoring Kayli while she dealt with her morning post. Kayli felt her insides clench uncomfortably.

She crossed and uncrossed her legs constantly until DCI Davis's gaze eventually locked with hers.

"Now, perhaps you'd care to tell me what the hell I walked in on this morning, Inspector? Is that man innocent or guilty of killing the victim?"

Kayli swallowed noisily. "At the time we arrested him, everything pointed to him carrying out the crime, ma'am."

"Everything? Care to enlighten me what you mean by that?" Davis sat back in her chair and picked up a pen which she began to tap on the pile of paperwork.

"We had proof that he was in the vicinity of the victim's flat via ANPR cameras. He's in the navy, ma'am, and is usually based in Plymouth, so we deemed that information to be a vital clue to the case."

"I see. I think I would come to the same conclusion given the evidence."

"I interviewed him with his solicitor last night. At first, he denied being anywhere near his ex-girlfriend's flat. Which raised my suspicions and led me to throwing him in the cell overnight while we awaited the DNA results. Unfortunately, they came back this morning and were negative."

"That is unfortunate. In that case, I can totally understand the man's anger. Especially if his mother was seriously injured in his absence."

"When we called at the address yesterday, I made sure the mother wasn't left alone. Mr. Young visited his neighbour and asked her to sit with his mother while he accompanied us to the station for questioning. I did everything by the book. I can only assume that the neighbour went about her business after a few hours and left the poor woman alone. I feel incredibly guilty about his mother taking a tumble, but there was very little I could have done to prevent it. I did my best in the circumstances. Maybe if Young had been honest with us from the outset, we wouldn't be in this mess now."

The DCI nodded and looked pensive. "This situation isn't going to go away. I believe he will live up to the threats he issued downstairs. Even more so if his mother dies."

Kayli held her head in shame. "Not sure I could have done things any differently, ma'am. My main priority was to try and get a killer off the streets ASAP. That kind of backfired on me."

Davis banged her hand on the desk, forcing Kayli to look up at her. "I will not have self-pitying in this room, Inspector. You did your job to the best of your ability, correct?"

"Yes, of course that's correct, ma'am." Davis's gaze held Kayli's for a long time, reaching deep into her soul. "Is there an inference in there that I'm missing, ma'am?"

Davis placed her pen on the desk then started clicking the thumb and forefinger together on her right hand. "How are things at home?"

Kayli raised a finger and wagged it from side to side. "No way. I refuse to let anyone pin this on me as if I've been distracted with my home life."

"Calm down. I wasn't inferring anything of the sort. I was merely asking the question. If it makes you feel any better, if I were in your shoes, I would be frantic, going out of my mind with worry."

"I am concerned about Mark. I'd be pretty heartless if I wasn't. It hits me more when I'm at home. Saying that, when I'm here, I give my all to the job, the same as I've always done, ma'am."

"Have you heard any news at all?"

"Nothing. My brother is dealing with the issue. He's in constant contact with the security firm out in Afghanistan. They're doing their best to try and find out where the bastards are keeping him—if Mark is still alive, that is—but they've heard nothing since he was abducted."

Davis shook her head. "That's appalling. I certainly feel for you, Inspector. Look, if you need time off to work through your emotions, don't hesitate to ask me. Are you due any holiday?"

"I'll be fine. I'd rather be here than at home. I have a couple of weeks outstanding that I need to use before the end of the year. I was hoping I could carry them over to next year if I don't use them up."

"We'll see. You know how I usually feel about that type of request. Sometimes it's hard enough squeezing five weeks holidays in, let alone carrying over any extra. You know head office's motto on that, 'use it or lose it'."

"I know. It was worth a shot. Maybe if we hear some good news about Mark, I can take a few weeks off when he finally comes home."

"Sounds like a great idea. Right, now bugger off and leave me to get on with my day."

Kayli smiled at the DCI and rose from her chair. "Thank you, ma'am. For backing me when I need it."

"Always. You're an excellent copper, Inspector. Now go find the person responsible for robbing that poor woman of her young life."

"Aye, aye, ma'am. I'm sure going to do my best. One last thing I need to bring to your attention, ma'am."

DCI Davis frowned. "Go on."

"Mr. Abel, the victim's father, is a solicitor."

"Well, that's just put the cherry on top. Okay, thanks for the warning."

Kayli left the room, feeling relieved that the meeting had gone better than she had anticipated. She made her way back to the incident room and called for the team's attention. "Listen up, guys. Looks like there is a storm brewing with regard to Mr. Young. He threatened all sorts downstairs—in front of the DCI, I hasten to add. That's where I've been, in her office, having the riot act read to me."

"What? You can't be serious?" Dave said, shaking his head in disgust.

"Deadly serious. Young is like a wounded animal, ready to lash out at anyone standing in his way. He has a right, I suppose. Although in my defence, I made sure his mother wasn't left alone at the property when we arrested him."

"That's it then. No need for you to be worried. Is the chief concerned by what she heard?"

"She says she isn't, but deep down, I'm not so sure."

"So, if he's innocent, where do we go from here?" Dave asked.

Kayli tucked a stray hair behind her ear and stared at the whiteboard, hoping to find inspiration. "We need to visit Sarah's workplace. A few things have come to light that need further investigation. The problems she had with a certain DJ, and also what Young witnessed—the kiss that took place between Sarah and Danny Talbot."

"Funny that he never mentioned that when we spoke to him previously," Dave said.

"Would you mention it if I showed my appreciation of you giving me a lift by kissing you on the cheek? He probably didn't think anything of it."

"You've got a point there although we don't know it was on the cheek."

CHAPTER SEVEN

The receptionist at the radio station greeted them with a glistening, toothy smile. "Hello there. How may I help you?"

Kayli flashed the redhead her warrant card. "We'd like to see the person in charge, if he's available?"

"Of course. Can I tell him what your visit is in connection with?"

"The death of one of your colleagues, Sarah Abel."

The woman's eyes nearly dropped out of her head, and her cheeks flushed with colour. "Yes, right away. Dreadful, dreadful incident."

The woman's hand shook as she placed the call to a Mr. Jackson. She hung up and smiled again. "He'll be with you in a second or two. Please, take a seat."

"Thanks, we'll stand. Did you know Sarah well?"

"Only in passing, really. We've had a few conversations over the years but nothing that in depth. Very sad that I won't see her cheerful disposition around here anymore. She was a lovely lady, always had a cheery smile. Hard to believe that she's no longer with us."

"We've heard nothing but good things about her. You didn't have any deep conversations about what might have been troubling her before her death then?"

"No. I wouldn't really say we were that close."

"That's a shame." Kayli made a circle with her finger and lowered her voice, "Nothing going on around here—with her male colleagues perhaps—that you can tell us about?"

The receptionist's mouth turned down at the sides, and she shook her head. "Not that I know of. Mr. Jackson will be able to fill you in more about that when you see him."

"Thanks."

A suited man with black hair going grey at the sides stepped out of an office and walked towards them. "I'm Harry Jackson. You wanted to see me?"

Hidden Agenda

Kayli showed him her ID. "DI Kayli Bright, and this invalid is my partner, DS Dave Chaplin," she replied, hoping to break the ice between them before she got down to the nitty-gritty questions that she had a feeling would be causing the man some discomfort.

"Pleased to meet you. Would you like to come through to my office?"

Kayli nodded, and she and Dave followed the man up the hallway. Pictures of several DJs wearing headphones, surrounded by equipment, adorned the walls. In his office, Mr. Jackson pulled another chair in front of the desk. Kayli sat down and waited for Dave to struggle into the seat beside her and ready his pen and notepad before she spoke. "Thank you for seeing us at such short notice. We really appreciate it, Mr. Jackson."

"You're welcome. I take it your visit here today means that you haven't caught the person who... took Sarah's life yet?"

Kayli shook her head. "No. Not yet. How well did you know Sarah?"

"As well as I know any of my staff, I suppose. Each of them have a particular role around the station, and if they do their job correctly, I tend to leave them to it. Only really pull them into the office if they're underperforming."

"By that, I take it you mean that Sarah was good at her job and you rarely had anything to do with her, right?"

"That's correct," he replied, sitting upright in his chair.

"Okay. Perhaps you can enlighten me about an incident that has come to our attention, involving Sarah and one of the DJs?"

His gaze drifted between her and Dave, and he chewed the inside of his mouth.

"Mr. Jackson? It would be better if you were honest with us. We could always conduct this interview down at the station if you'd rather?"

"No. Here is fine. I really don't want to drop any of my staff in the shit, Inspector."

"You won't be. May I remind you that we're conducting a murder enquiry? People's feelings really don't come into this. What do you know?"

His chest expanded as he inhaled a large breath, then he let it out slowly. "A few months ago, Sarah reported an incident, which I was forced to deal with."

"Go on." Kayli said.

"Sarah had a problem with one of our top DJs, accused him of touching her up."

Kayli raised an eyebrow. "Does that type of thing happen frequently, Mr. Jackson?"

He scratched the side of his face. "No, very rarely. I must admit I struggled to deal with the situation when the problem arose. Ryan is one of the station's stars."

"Ah, so you're telling me you were prepared to take his side rather than Sarah's. Am I right?"

"Not exactly. I think I dealt with the matter satisfactorily, if you must know," he replied defensively.

"You informed the police? Is that what you're telling me?"

"No. It never came to that. We dealt with things internally. To everyone's satisfaction."

"That's good to hear. May I ask how you reprimanded the DJ?"

"He was warned of his future conduct."

Kayli tilted her head. "I see... and was Sarah okay with that slight slap on the wrist for one of your *star* DJs?"

"Yes, in the end."

"In the end?"

He sighed. "The problem escalated before it got better. DJs are like actors, Inspector. They have egos that are super fragile and need to be handled delicately."

"I can understand that. However, if Sarah had a problem with one of her colleagues and you appeared to brush it under the carpet rather than deal with the issue adequately, then that could potentially cause more problems in the future."

He frowned. "I'm not with you."

"Let me clarify that for you: it could have caused the woman's death."

He shot forward in his chair. "No way! Ryan would never do such a thing."

"I'll need to question him myself before I can make a similar judgement, Mr. Jackson. Is he at work today?"

"Yes, he's on-air at the moment. Due to come off at around ten a.m."

"Good, not long to wait then. Perhaps you can tell me if Ryan has been in bother for this type of thing in the past, during his time at the station?"

His gaze drifted off to the left and Kayli instantly knew a lie was going to tumble out of his mouth.

"The truth would be nice, Mr. Jackson."

His neck darkened with crimson. "There was a similar incident recorded a few years ago, I seem to remember."

"And was Ryan 'warned of his future conduct' in that instance too?" Kayli asked, her eyes narrowing slightly.

"No."

"May I ask why?"

"Because the young girl left the station."

"Are you saying that she resigned or that you sacked her?"

Jackson puffed out his cheeks and shrugged. "No, she resigned. However, she caused such a stink about the incident that it was borderline whether I sacked her or not. She was the total opposite to Sarah in character. Sarah was willing to let me handle the situation, whereas Becky went down another route and got her brothers involved. She and her brothers cornered Ryan in the car park one night and gave him a good seeing-to."

"And yet he didn't seem to learn from his mistake. He still tried it on with Sarah."

"I have no idea what goes on in other people's minds, Inspector. Like I said, he was warned of his future conduct, and that was the end of it."

"Okay, I can see that we're going around in circles here. Do I have your permission to question Ryan after his stint on the air has finished?"

"If it's acceptable to him, then yes. Forgive me, I'm not trying to be difficult here. I run a happy ship most of the time and find it very uncomfortable when things become unbalanced because a member of staff has stepped out of line."

"I appreciate your candour. Any other incidences that we should know about concerning Sarah Abel?"

He shook his head. "Not that I can think of, no. Should there be?"

"Just asking the question, Mr. Jackson. Would you give us permission to speak to all the members of your staff while we're here? Just in case they're aware of anything we might find useful that you're unaware of."

Jackson shrugged. "Why not? Although I'm pretty sure that no other problems have occurred that I'm unaware of."

"Is there a room we can use to interview people?"

"Yes, next door, there's a conference room we use for our daily meetings. I'll instruct the staff to come and see you one by one. Do you want to start with anyone in particular?"

Kayli smiled. "That's very helpful, thank you. No, however you want to do things is fine by me. We're willing to let your staff go about their normal duties during our time here. All right if we get things underway now? Time is of the essence, after all, and we have a killer to find."

He left his chair and rushed out the door.

Kayli and Dave waited patiently for him to return a few moments later. "Everything is set up. There are seven members of staff on site at present. Some of them are dealing with what's going out on-air right now, but if you don't mind waiting around, they've all agreed to see you."

"Excellent news." Kayli helped Dave with his crutches, and they repositioned themselves in the office next door.

Jackson held open the door for them. "Make yourselves at home. Tammy said she'd like to go first, to get it over with. I'll send her in."

"Thanks, that'll be great."

Jackson closed the door.

"What do you make of him? A bit shifty in my book," Dave pointed out as soon as they were alone.

"Not sure. He comes across as though he's the type who finds it hard to deal with difficult circumstances, such as a harassment charge. But who knows? Make sure you get everyone's name down correctly and we'll do thorough checks on all of them when we're back at the station."

"Will do. I must say I'm rather keen to hear what this superstar DJ has to say for himself."

"Me too. Do you know him?"

Dave shook his head and lowered his voice. "To be honest with you, I find this station's music kind of trashy. They're not exactly with the times. Stuck in a rut and only tend to play music from the eighties and nineties."

Kayli chuckled. "Get you. I didn't realise you were 'down and with it' and prefer the music of today battering your eardrums."

He closed his eyes and tilted his head from side to side. "If you must know, I have a super-eclectic taste in music. I quite often have opera playing at dinner parties in my house."

"Ooo... get you. Of course, I wouldn't know that, having not attended one of your soirées before."

"Ouch, sorry. Maybe we can rectify that when Mark comes home."

She sighed and mumbled, "If he comes home. Crap, did you have to mention his name? I was doing well this morning."

"Sorry. I've got your back if the questions dry up," he replied as the door opened and a young girl with spiky red hair, wearing dungarees entered the room.

"Hi, I'm Tammy Colt. You wanted to see me?"

"Yes. Why don't you take a seat, Tammy?"

"I know this is about Sarah, and can I just say before we start how devastated we all were to learn of her... death?"

"It is appalling. However, our intention is to make the person who did this pay for that crime by putting them behind bars. Now, what can you tell us about Sarah?"

"What's there to tell, except that she was a really nice person and that she'll be missed around here?"

"Did you know her long?"

"A couple of years. She sort of took me under her wing when I first started here. She was a very kind person. Why would anyone kill someone that kind?"

"We don't have all the answers yet. First, we have to pin down the culprit. Hopefully, they'll be able to enlighten us. By what people have told us about Sarah's character so far, it's hard for us to fathom. Tell me, did you know much about the problems she had with one of the DJs?"

Tammy's gaze dropped to the table, and she nodded. "A little bit. She was very evasive about it, although when I saw the two of them together, the air became very frosty between them."

"Are we talking about the same person? Was it Ryan?"

"I believe so. Ryan Wilson."

"Can I ask if either you or any of the other female staff have had a similar problem with this Ryan?" Kayli heard the young woman swallow and sensed a denial coming next. "It's okay, you can be as honest as you want to be in this room. We have no intention of dropping anyone in it, if that's what you're concerned about, and it will aid our investigation. Someone with malice killed your colleague, and we need to question any likely suspects."

"I understand. He touched me up once, not long after I heard that Sarah had put in a complaint to the boss."

"Interesting. How did you respond to his unwanted advance?"

She shrugged. "I'm a bit feisty when someone touches me like that. I grabbed hold of his hand and bent his fingers back. Told him if he ever touched me inappropriately again, I'd make sure my boxer brother knew where he lived."

Kayli smiled at the woman's ballsy behaviour. "Do you have a brother? I'm sensing not."

"No. But it did the trick. I don't think I've been alone in a room with him since."

"He doesn't sound all that brave to me," Dave piped up.

"I don't think he is. Probably one of these pricks—excuse my language—that takes satisfaction in flouting his status to get what he wants from a woman," Tammy replied.

"Do you know if he has a regular girlfriend? Or if he's on the lookout for one?"

"I don't know. Not heard anything either way on the grapevine. Saying that, I think if he had a girlfriend, he wouldn't treat women that way... or would he? I bat for the other side, if you know what I mean. Mainly because I can never figure out what goes on in a man's head." Grinning at Dave, she added, "No offence."

"None taken. In my defence, I'm not like normal men. My boss can vouch for me there." Dave glanced at Kayli.

She raised her eyebrows at him. "Moving on..." She chuckled. "No, seriously, he's a good man. His fiancée and son seem to think he's all right, anyway."

Dave looked mortified until Kayli winked at him. He shook his head and glanced down, ready to take more notes.

"Do you think any of the other female staff members have had similar interactions with him? Or do you think after you reprimanded him he's mended his ways?"

"Hard to say. Maybe they'll confide in you when you question them. Do you think he's the one?"

"Who killed Sarah?"

Tammy nodded, her eyes wide with expectation.

"I doubt it. Sounds to me like he's a chancer, but nowadays, all murderers don't come from the same mould. It only takes one minor incident to trigger someone's anger, and bam! Another victim ends up on the slab in the mortuary."

"Do you think that's due to people being angrier these days? I witness at least two road rage episodes on the way home from work every night."

"It's hard to say what triggers people's anger. All I know is that crime rates are escalating, and the reasons why they're rising are becoming more and more bizarre with each passing day."

"That's so sad. I guess we should all be more vigilant going forward then."

Kayli nodded. "I'd certainly advise it, especially to women. Getting back to Sarah, do you think she had any problems with anyone else around here?"

"I don't recall hearing anything. We all tend to get on really well as a group. Just the odd dickhead, like Ryan, who chances his arm trying to screw things up."

"Okay, then I'd like to thank you for sparing us the time. You've been really helpful."

Tammy smiled. "Only speaking up for a friend. Do your best to find the culprit, Inspector. Sarah was so young. It's not right that someone should rob her of her life and be allowed to get away with it."

"You have my word that we'll do everything in our power not to let that happen."

Over the next half an hour, Kayli and Dave interviewed the rest of the staff. Two more women came across as being very cagey when voicing their concerns about any possible sexual harassment that might have come their way. While the men couldn't understand what the line of questioning was all about, each of them had assured Kayli that they had never witnessed any form of harassment at the station.

That left two people they needed to speak to, Ryan Wilson and Danny Talbot. The next person to saunter into the room was the bigshot DJ himself. As soon as she laid eyes on Ryan Wilson, Kayli's hackles on the back of her neck stood to attention. He had blond hair, which he probably dyed to make himself look younger. But upon closer inspection, the crow's feet around his vivid blue eyes gave away his real age.

Kayli introduced herself and Dave. "Hello, Mr. Wilson. Thank you for dropping by to see us. This shouldn't take long."

"Please, call me Ryan. Everyone does." He fell into his chair and casually placed one leg over the other, his right ankle resting on his left knee.

In Kayli's eyes he oozed cockiness and she found herself searching for ways to bring the jerk down. She sensed Dave getting agitated beside her too. "Very well, Ryan. Are you aware of why we are here today?"

"There's a rumour circulating that you're on the lookout for Sarah Abel's killer. You seriously think any of us would be capable of doing that, Inspector?"

"Well, someone killed her. This is the obvious place to start. Wouldn't you agree, Ryan?"

"No. Not at all. But then I ain't a copper with a suspicious mind."

Kayli chewed the inside of her mouth, trying to keep her temper in check. She could tell he was going to be a tough cookie to handle and was suddenly glad she'd brought Dave along instead of Donna. "If we didn't possess suspicious minds, half the crimes committed in the UK would remain unsolved."

He shrugged. "I suppose. Anyway, what can I do to help? I was shocked when I heard what had happened to Sarah. She was a lovely girl."

"We keep hearing that. Obviously, the killer didn't have the same impression of her. Otherwise she wouldn't have been brutally murdered."

"I wasn't aware her death was brutal. What happened?" Ryan asked, tapping his fingers on his ankle.

"We're not at liberty to divulge the details. What we have gleaned from the other staff members is that you had a problem with Sarah. Care to tell us about that, Ryan?" She smiled as he dropped his foot to the floor and fidgeted in his chair.

"I think someone has been telling you lies, Inspector."

"Have they? Your boss was the first to fill us in on the harassment charge Sarah laid at your door. Are you calling *him* a liar?"

He flung his arms out to the side then ran a shaking hand through his wavy hair. "All right. I might have tried it on with her once. I thought she gave me the come-on. It was a genuine mistake, and I regretted my actions immediately."

"Really? Only we heard that not long after the incident with Sarah, you tried it on with another female member of staff. Do you have a problem keeping your urges under control, Mr. Wilson?"

"No, I frigging do not. Some of these girls should be grateful that someone makes their day for them. It's not like they're raving stunners fighting off other men."

Kayli tutted. "*Grateful*? What type of logic is that? Are you saying that all women should be happy if you deign to show them any form of attention?"

"Yeah, like I said, they should appreciate it."

"Doesn't that thought process belong in the Stone Age, Mr. Wilson?"

"No, not at all."

"May I ask if you are in a permanent relationship at present?"

Ryan fidgeted even more before he answered. "I started seeing someone a couple of weeks ago, if you must know."

"Perhaps you can tell me how you'd feel if your steady girlfriend confided in you that someone at work was harassing her?"

He ground his teeth and shook his head. "I'd be livid and want to smash the bloke in the face."

"Strange reaction, considering you were accused of doing the very same thing around here, Ryan, don't you think?"

His eyes narrowed. He looked at Dave for help then back at Kayli. "I get your point. Never really thought about it before."

"I'm glad to see you being so remorseful, even if it is too late for Sarah to witness."

"I said that I regretted my actions immediately, Inspector. What more can I say?"

"And yet you went on to harass another staff member within a few weeks. That kind of behaviour doesn't sound very remorseful to me. Maybe I'm missing something?" Kayli turned to face her partner. "Can you help me out with this, Dave?"

He shook his head. "I'm inclined to agree with you, boss. Disgraceful behaviour and one that in the past has led to worse crimes."

"Whoa! Now wait just a second. I didn't kill Sarah, if that's what you're bloody implying."

"We weren't, but thank you for pointing that out. Any idea where Sarah lived?"

"Nope. Should I have?"

"I just wondered if you or any of your colleagues had visited her flat."

"No. We don't tend to socialise as a group that often, only at Christmas. I wouldn't know where she lived."

"Okay. Did you ever see her being friendly with anyone else at the station?"

He fell silent for a moment. "Only Danny Talbot. I think he used to give her a lift home when she was in dire straits. Always seemed pretty keen to help Sarah out, if you know what I mean." He tapped the side of his nose.

"Are you insinuating that he liked her?"

"I think he more than liked her. Not sure if it went anywhere, though. I think Sarah had recently split up from her fella. Hey, have you had a word with him? You know what it's like when someone gets jilted. Maybe *he* killed her. I heard he's in the navy. His training would give him access to ways of killing people in combat, wouldn't it?"

"We've already questioned and released him. We're satisfied that he had nothing to do with her death."

"Then I don't envy you guys trying to find the killer. Have you considered this being a burglary that went wrong?"

"Thanks for the advice. That's yet another scenario we're looking into. If you have nothing else to add, then I think we're done here, Ryan."

He leapt out of his chair and reached across the table to shake their hands. "It's been a pleasure chatting to you both. Give me a ring if you want a special request read out over the airwaves any time... umm... personal not professional, of course."

Kayli shook his hand and resisted the temptation to instantly wipe her palm down her trousers as she watched him walk out of the room.

"What an effing creep," Dave muttered.

Kayli laughed and shuddered. "You took the words right out of my mouth. I'm not getting the impression that he should be treated as a suspect, though, are you?"

"Nope. All he's guilty of is being a grade-one tosser with wandering-hand trouble."

Kayli stood up and held on to the back of Dave's chair so he could get to his feet easily. "Back to the station then, I suppose."

As they left the room, Kayli spotted Danny Talbot. She dug her partner in the ribs as they walked up the hallway. "Hello, Danny. How's it going?"

The young man spun around, looking surprised to see them. "Oh, hi. I didn't know you were here. Everything all right?"

"Yes, just following up on a few things in our investigation."

"I take it you haven't arrested anyone yet?"

"Not yet. But we're getting close."

His eyes widened. "That's great news. I hope you arrest someone soon. I must fly. The boss is expecting me," he said, turning towards Jackson's office.

"Nice seeing you again. Oh, wait—one question if I may before you disappear?"

He halted and faced her, smiling broadly. "What's that?"

Kayli took a step closer to him and looked over her shoulder to make sure the receptionist was occupied. "You neglected to tell us that when you dropped Sarah off the other night, she kissed you before she left the car."

He leaned back as a frown appeared. "Should I have? Did someone tell you that? Was someone spying on me?"

"Calm down. I think you should have informed us, just in case any of your DNA showed up on Sarah's body."

His hand covered his face. "Oh God, I never thought about that. I'm so sorry. It wasn't intentional, I promise you. Who told you?"

"I'd like to keep that information to myself for now. Let's just say that someone spotted you dropping Sarah off at her flat."

"Did this mystery person also tell you that I drove off right away once she'd left my car?"

"No. They didn't tell us that because they left the scene immediately after witnessing the kiss between you."

"Between us? She kissed me on the cheek as a thank you. I feel very uncomfortable that someone placed me at the scene, Inspector."

"Why? You volunteered that information yourself, as I seem to recall."

"If someone is trying to put me in the frame for her murder, then I think I have a right to know who that person is."

She shook her head. "No one is insinuating you had anything to do with Sarah's murder. All I was saying is that you should have told us that she kissed you, especially as you were one of the last people to see her alive."

"It sounds like a roundabout way of accusing me, if you don't mind me saying."

"I wasn't. I'm sorry if it came across that way."

"Apology accepted. I need to hurry now, or the boss will be using my knackers as a paperweight."

Kayli chuckled. "Thanks for sparing us the time."

"No problem. Always glad to help the police with their enquiries."

Kayli and Dave returned to the car. "This is so frustrating. Are you sure we did the right thing in releasing the boyfriend?" Dave asked, one hand on the roof of the car as he placed his crutches inside the vehicle.

"No. But what can we do when the DNA fails to place him at the scene? Our hands are tied when that happens—you know that."

"I know. But what other options are open to us? Maybe it was a damn burglary gone wrong after all."

"I'm at a loss, Dave. My head is all over the place on this one, and worrying about Mark isn't helping. I know I try and not think about his situation at work, but I just can't help wondering if my personal life is affecting the choices I'm making during this investigation." She placed her head on the steering wheel.

Dave prodded her upper arm. "Bloody hell, you don't half talk a lot of shit for an inspector at times."

She sat back in her seat and turned to look at him, her mouth turned down at the sides. "Do I? I'm bound to doubt myself at times."

"There's having niggling doubts, which we all get in this job, and there's talking utter bullshit. You, in my honest opinion, are talking the latter."

She laughed. "Well, I guess that's me told then."

Kayli started the car and drove off. She was still riddled with self-doubt as they walked into the incident room. Donna and Graeme both looked their way. Kayli shook her head. "Nothing, guys. Not one thing. What about you?"

"The same, boss. All the background checks we've carried out have thrown up nothing useful. Not sure where we should be turning next," Donna replied, appearing to be downbeat, which wasn't like her at all.

"Hey, keep the faith, Donna. We'll do some brainstorming after we've had a revitalising cup of coffee and go from there."

"Yes, boss."

Graeme leapt out of his chair and approached the vending machine. "I'll get these for a change."

Kayli stumbled against the nearest desk. "Crikey! We'll need to chalk this one up, guys. Have you won the lottery or something, Graeme?"

He tutted. "No. I should be offended by that remark. I do put my hand in my pocket occasionally, boss."

"Very occasionally," Dave muttered behind his hand.

They all laughed. It was good to relieve the tension now and again. After their drink, they revisited the case, trying to find the missing piece of the puzzle that would lead them to the killer.

Kayli clicked her fingers. "Sarah's phone. Donna, did you manage to get the call information from it yet?"

"Damn, I knew there was something I needed to chase up. I'll get onto that now, boss."

"Brilliant. I don't remember seeing her phone at the crime scene. I'm going to ring the pathologist to see if her guys picked it up." She strode into her office to make the call. Naomi answered the phone herself. "Hi, Naomi. It's Kayli. Just a quick one. I was wondering if you picked up Sarah Abel's mobile phone at the flat."

"Oh, hi. I was going to ring you in a little while. Let me check the evidence sheet."

Kayli could hear rustling paper and tapped her pen on the desk as she waited for Naomi to come back on the line.

"Ah, yes, here's the sheet. Nope, we haven't got it. Can't say I noticed it at the flat, either."

"Okay, that might help our investigation then. Thanks for that. Why were you going to ring me?"

"I have the PM results for you."

"Okay, I'm all ears. What was the cause of death?"

"Asphyxiation. Although as I suspected, she would have drowned in her own vomit had she not been suffocated first."

"Poor girl. Nothing else?"

"Yes, something interesting showed up when I examined all the items she was wearing. Her clothes had vomit on them also."

"That figures."

"No. It didn't seep from the bag. I'm presuming she vomited before the bag was put over her head. Which means—"

"That when we find the killer, there should be sick on his clothing, right?"

"Spot on. Providing he hasn't washed the clothes by now, of course. But there's more."

Kayli's heart rate intensified as she picked up on the excitement in Naomi's tone. "Go on. Surprise me."

"The victim was wearing a metal watch strap."

"And?"

"Within the watch strap, I found a few hairs."

"Interesting. I take it you've compared the hairs to Sarah's DNA, and they're not a match."

"You are correct. I also compared them to the DNA we collected from your prime suspect, and the DNA didn't match his, either."

"So we need to find who those hairs belong to, right?"

"We do. My team are running different tests and have put the information through the system. Unfortunately, we haven't established any results as yet, but if we find anything, you'll be the first to know."

"Okay, that might not seem much at this stage, but it could turn the investigation on its head soon enough. You've definitely brightened my day. The case was beginning to get me and my team down, not that we've had much sleep in the last few days."

"Ditto. It's lucky we love our jobs, right?"

Kayli laughed. "Sometimes I doubt that's true, like today. We seem to be going round and round in circles and not getting far with this one."

"Something will click into place soon enough. Just be patient. Are you taking tomorrow off?"

"Yeah, I think so. I'm hoping Mum and Dad will invite me to have dinner with them. I hate being at the house by myself... you know, without Mark being there."

"Any news on that front?"

"No, nothing. It's as though he's just vanished."

"Stay strong. No news and all that."

"I'm trying, I promise. Daft bloody adages like that don't help, either. How can people not worry just because there's no news?"

Naomi chuckled. "I know. I shouldn't have said anything. I reiterate, you should remain strong and positive at all times. That's all you can do really."

"I'm trying. Although I'm tempted to bloody go out there myself and bring him home."

"Bloody hell! The Taliban would definitely run for the hills with you on their patch." Naomi sniggered.

Kayli laughed at the thought of seeing turban-clad men being terrified of her. "I better go. We need to try and trace this damn phone. Thanks for the info. Can you email me the report for the file?"

"I will. Take care. Try and have a restful Sunday."

"You too. Speak soon." Kayli hung up and sat back in her chair. She glanced out the window at the greying sky and saw Mark's handsome face etched into a cloud as it drifted past the window. *Be safe, Mark. I'd be there in a shot if I could. Always know that you're not far from my thoughts and that there are people out there searching for you. Remain positive. I love you.*

She shook the sad thoughts from her head, preferring to concentrate on the case, and stepped back into the incident room. "Any news, Donna?"

"Yes, boss. Apparently, they sent the records to the wrong email address. I have them now. Just going to print them out for you."

"Brilliant news. I'm not saying they'll break the case for us, but at this point, we have very little to go on anyway. The pathologist has told me that she found hairs in Sarah's watch strap. And no, they didn't belong to either the victim or Young. She's still running the DNA through the database. Hopefully, something will come of that soon. The phone was not found at the scene. So someone has it... it's too much of a coincidence to think she lost it just before her death. We need to trace that phone. Dave, you've got a friend in the tech department, haven't you?"

Dave nodded and pointed at her. "I do. I'll get on to him now. Tell him it's urgent and we need the results ASAP."

"Brilliant. Let's hope he can help us out."

"He will. Not sure the weekend is going to help, though." He got on the phone right away and shook his head.

"No go?" Kayli asked as soon as he hung up.

"Nope. He's got another urgent job on the go. The earliest he can get to it is Monday."

"Monday will have to do then. Let's not get downbeat about this, guys. We still have Sarah's phone records to go through."

Kayli pulled up a chair alongside Donna, and together, they went through the pages of calls Sarah Abel had made the week prior to her death.

"Let's start ringing some of these numbers, see who these people are, Donna. You start from the beginning of the list, and I'll work backwards with the most recent calls."

Before either of them could place a call, Dave cleared his throat as if he wanted to say something.

"Don't be shy, partner. Spit it out."

"Maybe you should be careful ringing those numbers in case one of them belongs to the killer."

Kayli pushed the sheet of paper away as if it had just seared her hand. "Bloody hell, you're right, Dave. Any chance your guy can find out who the numbers belong to as well for us?"

"I'm sure he can do that. Maybe the killer took the phone to cover his tracks."

"Or maybe he took it for a trophy. I think we need to see if any cases similar to this have been reported in the area in the last few months, or years, before we go any further. Sorry, guys, I've let you down. I should have instructed you to delve into that from the kick-off." Kayli sighed and shook her head.

"What a load of codswallop you talk at times. This case has been different from the get-go, boss. We dealt with it within minutes of the crime being carried out, during the golden hour. We're not always able to do that. Therefore, our investigation spun off in a different direction, and our priority was to pick Young up," Dave said, annoyance apparent in his tone.

"I agree with Dave on this one, boss," Graeme chipped in.

Kayli looked at Donna, who was nodding and smiling. "I also agree. You could never let us down, boss."

Kayli sniffled as her eyes became moist with tears. "You really are the best team an inspector has ever had the fortune of having by their side. Look, let's do what we can, researching other crimes in the area, then call it a day around four, okay? We deserve a break after the hours we've put in over the last few days. We need to recharge our batteries and hit the ground running again on Monday."

Dave shrugged. "Sounds good to me."

Each of them sat behind a monitor and carried out a search. Kayli decided to go back five years in her search, but after a few hours of mind-numbing research, she sat back in her chair and expelled a large breath. "Nothing. What about you guys?"

The other three members of her team all shook their heads.

"Not one thing," Dave said, throwing his hands up in the air.

"Okay, let's remain positive. Maybe it vindicates my decision not to go down that route sooner, which makes me feel a whole lot better. Come on, I insist we should call it a day."

CHAPTER EIGHT

Exhaustion overwhelmed Kayli the second she entered her home. She went through to the kitchen, searched the cupboards, and removed a can of tomato soup from the shelf. Ten minutes later, she was sitting at the kitchen table dunking a piece of toast in her bowl of soup. After she finished, she plucked up the courage to ring her parents. "Hello, Mum. Sorry I haven't rung lately. It's been a hectic few days at work."

"It's all right, love. I accept that you're busy. Glad you're able to take your mind off things, you know."

"I know. I'm fine while I'm at work. It tends to hit me when I come home, though. I hate being here by myself. I keep expecting to find Mark sitting on the couch, annoying me by flicking through the channels. When I'm in the bedroom, all I can smell is his aftershave around me. That sets me off."

"It's bound to, darling. Why don't you come and stay with us until he comes home?"

"Thanks for the invite, Mum, but it wouldn't feel right leaving the house for some reason. Would it be all right if I invite myself to dinner tomorrow, though? I'm sure one of your stunning Sunday roasts will go down a treat and put the world to rights again."

"Of course. We've got a nice piece of topside for tomorrow. Come for a one o'clock dinner?"

"I'll probably come earlier, if that's all right? I can help prepare the veg."

"Whatever you want to do is fine by me, darling. If you're lonely this evening and fancy a chat, just give us a call."

"I will. Thanks, Mum. I love you."

"I love you too, dear."

As soon as Kayli hung up, sadness descended and wrapped around her shoulders. She decided she needed a soak in the bath. She poured a glass of wine and took it upstairs to run the bath. After a long, luxurious soak, she dried her hair then got into bed, even though it was only six thirty. Before long, she was engrossed in her new Linda Prather thriller, *The 13th Victim*—that was until her Kindle hit her on the forehead because she'd dozed off. She settled down under the warm duvet and drifted off to sleep. It wasn't long before she found herself dreaming about Mark. This time, she was transported to the desert. She could hear his faint cries for help as she approached an old wooden door that was secured by a large padlock. "Mark, I'm here. Hang tight. We'll get you out."

"Kayli? Kayli, is that you? They're starving me to death." His weak voice touched her heart.

"It's me, darling. You're safe now. We've come to rescue you."

"You don't understand! Be careful. There's a—"

She woke up with a start, drenched in a cold sweat. With tears trickling down her cheeks, she looked at the clock beside her. It was only three o'clock in the morning. She spent the next few hours tossing and turning, fighting her fears about Mark's safety, and feeling useless because she was unable to help him. For the first time in years, she resorted to praying.

Kayli finally got up to make herself a mug of coffee at six thirty. She paced the kitchen floor, waiting for the kettle to boil. The image of Mark, chained up somewhere and left to die the most unimaginable death possible, ran continuously through her tired mind. "I doubt I'm ever going to sleep again. How can I? Knowing that he's out there, in need of my help?"

She waited until eight o'clock then rang Giles. She felt guilty when his groggy voice answered her call. "This better be good, sis. It's Sunday, after all."

Kayli chewed her bottom lip. "I'm sorry. Go back to sleep." She hung up.

Her mobile rang seconds later. "Don't do that to me. You obviously rang me for a reason. What's wrong?"

"I'm sorry, Giles, please forgive me. Hey, just be grateful I didn't ring you at three, when I first woke up. At least I left it until it was a decent hour."

"Eight on a Sunday is a decent hour? Not in my book, love. What's wrong... as if I didn't know?"

Kayli let out a shuddering breath as she struggled to fight back the tears. "I'm worried—no, more than that—I'm petrified for

Mark's safety. Are you sure the guys out there are doing their best for him?"

"Christ, I hope you never get the chance to meet them if you think that, love. Of course they are. If they knew you were doubting their abilities, they would be mortally offended. He's one of their own. A soldier never really leaves the forces. These men will be going above and beyond to find out where he's being kept. It's a *vast* country. You have no idea what the terrain is like over there. And you know our guys are going to stick out like sore thumbs amongst the locals."

"I know. I'm not really doubting their abilities. It's just that I dreamt about Mark last night, and he said they were starving him to death. He's been missing two weeks now. If they're not feeding him, he won't have long left. I thought I read somewhere that a body can't survive without food for longer than two weeks."

"Your research is wrong, love. A body can survive for up to three weeks without food. Without water is another story entirely."

"Crap! What's that?"

"Less than a week, in most cases."

Kayli gasped. "No! I didn't realise that. In other words, you think he might already be dead?"

"I didn't say that, sis. I doubt it. Look, I'll see if I can contact the team searching for him today. It'll have to be later, though." His voice went to a whisper. "Annabelle has been up half the night. This pregnancy has hit her badly this time."

"What has the doctor said?"

"That if she doesn't stop being sick soon, they'll have to take her into hospital."

"Oh shit. Giles, I'm sorry for burdening you with my silly concerns at a time like this. You go. Give my love to Annabelle and Bobby."

"I will, and please stop worrying. I'm just as concerned about my best friend as you are. Try and put it out of your mind. There's no point dwelling on something that's beyond your control. You're only going to make yourself ill. You're going to Mum and Dad's for dinner today, aren't you?"

"I'm supposed to be."

"You can't let them down now, Kayli."

"The last thing I want to be is a down in the mouth around them. As you can imagine, I haven't got a lot to smile about at the moment, what with this frustrating case I'm working on and with Mark still being missing."

"Nonsense. They'll understand. Mum's a good listener, and that's what you need right now. It'll do you good to talk about things rather than let them fester."

"Maybe you're right. I wish you guys were going to be there today."

"It's just not possible with Annabelle feeling under the weather. I have to go now. I can hear Bobby calling out for his mum, and she's still in the bathroom, wrapped around the loo."

"Okay, thanks for chatting. Sorry I woke you so early. Ring me if there is anything I can do to help."

"I will. Take care of yourself and open up to Mum and Dad, for God's sake. Love you lots."

"All right. Thanks for chatting. Love you lots too." She hung up, feeling a little better.

Then she thought over her brother's words about surviving without the necessities in life. Maybe her dream had revealed Mark's final words to her. Perhaps he was dead now. Fresh tears filled her eyes, and she broke down and really sobbed for the first time in her life. Until now, her life had been filled with a lot of happiness. Sadness and black days had evaded her until Mark had come out of the army. Although they weren't married, she and Mark lived together as man and wife, and she was finding it difficult to exist without him by her side. Drying her eyes, she jumped in the shower then slipped on a clean pair of jeans and a pullover. She left her home at ten o'clock and drove to her parents' house.

Her mother squeezed her tightly when she walked into the kitchen. "Hello, darling. You're early, not that I'm complaining." She held Kayli away from her and shook her head. "You look dreadful. You haven't been looking after yourself at all."

Kayli hugged her mother again. "Don't be silly. I'm fine. Overworked and a little stressed out, but that's nothing unusual in my job. You know that."

Her mother turned away and withdrew a few pots from the cupboard before she moved over to the fridge to extract the vegetables that needed preparing for their meal. "We can natter and work at the same time. Your father has nipped out to the shops as I didn't have any ice cream in the freezer for pudding."

"You needn't have gone overboard, Mum."

"I haven't. This is our usual roast dinner. It's a shame Giles and Annabelle couldn't join us."

"I rang Giles first thing, I woke him up actually. He said that Annabelle is finding this pregnancy really tough. How is it that some people breeze through pregnancy while others have the life sucked out of them? I don't profess to know the workings of the body in such instances, but the thought of spending most of my day throwing up is enough to put me off having kids for life."

"I don't know. It depends on your hormone levels, I think. I'm not an expert on that side of things as I was one of those who breezed through my pregnancies when I was carrying you and Giles. If you want children, don't let Annabelle's experience put you off." She clicked her fingers. "I bet she'll be right as rain in a week or so."

"I hope so, for her sake. I wish I could do more to help..."

"But you have your own problems to deal with. Is that what you were about to say, darling?"

Kayli smiled at her intuitive mother. "No flies on you, Mum."

"I'm sure Mark will be fine, sweetheart. Did Giles mention if the team out there had any news regarding where these evil men are keeping him?"

"No, nothing. I dreamt about Mark last night. He was pleading for us to help him."

Her mother gathered her in her arms as the tears began to fall once more. After a few moments' comfort, Kayli pulled away and dried her eyes on a nearby tea towel.

"I know how hard it must be for you, sweetheart. Lord knows your father has had his share of fighting in dangerous situations over the years, during his army days."

"How did you cope, Mum?"

She shrugged her ageing shoulders. "You just do, lovely. It's what army wives are expected to do. Hey, I've had days when I've been gravely concerned about you over the years too. Your job is right up there in the danger stakes, and yet, look how capable you are at dealing with the trauma et cetera that is flung at you on a daily basis."

Kayli smiled and kissed her mother on the cheek. "How come you always know the right things to say?"

"Because I'm a mother. It's inbuilt from the day I felt you growing inside."

She chuckled. "I believe you."

They heard her father enter the front door. Kayli rushed into his arms the minute she saw him.

"Hey, what's all this? Not that I'm complaining. I'll have all the cuddles you ladies want to throw at me. I'm not fussy. Can't afford to be at my time of life."

Kayli took a step back. "Idiot. The thing is, I don't tell either of you enough how much I love you. You've been rocks for me over the years, and I'll be forever grateful for the sacrifices you've made to raise Giles and me in difficult circumstances."

Her father put the ice cream he'd just bought in the freezer then threw an arm around Kayli's shoulder. "It's all part of the parenting process. To be there when our children need us the most. We're lucky to have two incredibly intelligent children in you and Giles. It was never a chore bringing you up. Always a genuine pleasure."

"Thanks, Dad. That means a lot. If we have time later, can I bend your ear about a few things?"

Her father frowned. "Such as?"

"Just things in general," she said evasively.

"Of course. You know I'm always here for you if you need to run anything past me."

"I'll help Mum with the veg first, and then we can have a chat, if that's okay?"

"That's a deal. I'll be in the study until then. Bring a coffee with you when you come."

Kayli laughed. "I know where I get my love of coffee from, that's for sure."

After preparing the sprouts, red cabbage and green beans while her mother peeled the potatoes and parsnips to get them ready for roasting, Kayli boiled the kettle and made them all a coffee. "Why don't you put your feet up for half an hour in the lounge, Mum?"

"I think I'll do just that, dear. Enjoy your time with your father. I have an idea what the discussion is going to be about."

"That's because you're an extremely smart lady."

Kayli eased her father's study door open. "Is it safe to come in? You don't have any official papers on show?"

"Don't be daft. Those days are behind me now, love. Come in and sit down. Thanks for the coffee."

Kayli set the mugs down on the edge of his leather desktop. "Thanks for this, Dad."

"You know my door is always open for you. What's on your mind? As if I couldn't guess."

"How did you cope, Dad? You were captured by the enemy in your early days in the army, I seem to remember."

"I was. A small conflict we got involved in out in Thailand. However, luck was on our side back then when a few of us managed to overwhelm our captors one day."

"Wow, I didn't know that. How did you escape?"

"How? There were six of us. The idiots left one man guarding us. One of our guys pretended to be ill. The little guard panicked, asked us what to do. I told him to untie the soldier so that he wasn't restricted. The fool did just that. As soon as his hands were untied, the soldier knocked him unconscious and released the rest of us. We escaped into the hills before our captors could return. We watched them arrive. They slapped around the guard who was put in charge of us for a while before one of the bastards shot him in the head. My team and I were mortified, riddled with guilt for days as we tracked through the jungle to civilisation and our freedom. It was one of the worst periods of my life. Luckily, I had your mother, you and Giles to think about—I had to get home to be with you. That determination saw me through that tortuous ordeal, love."

Kayli grabbed his hand. "That's reassuring to know, Dad. I hope the same grit and determination is within Mark to keep the faith. My dream last night was so vivid, I fear that he isn't going to make it through this."

"He will. He's a determined critter. Giles is confident that the team will find him soon. Don't lose heart, sweetheart. These are experienced, resolute men trying to find him. I'm sure they won't let Mark down. Give them time."

"But in my dream, he spoke to me, told me that they were starving him to death. If that's true, then who knows what condition he will be in when they find him, or even if he will still be alive by then? I'm not sure what I'll do without him, Dad."

"Nonsense. Stop being so negative now. Do you hear me?"

Kayli nodded. "I'm trying. But fear keeps swooping down and consuming me."

"You wouldn't be human if you didn't feel that way about someone you loved. Let's not dwell on what ifs and maybes, okay? If he's still alive—and at this point, there's no reason to assume otherwise—then I'm sure it will only be a few days or weeks before you two are reunited. And when you are, I hope for your sake, you can persuade him to give up his dangerous career. If he needs to find work in this country, I'll do everything I can to see he secures a decent job. You have my word on that."

Kayli leaned forward and hugged her father, clinging to his neck for a long time. "Thanks, Dad," she whispered through her tears. "That means a lot."

"Now, enough talk about what is out of our hands. Tell me all about the case you're working on. By the looks of you, it seems to be taking a toll."

She pulled away and sat back in her chair. "I'm fine. No need to worry about me. The case is one of the most frustrating I've had to deal with in my career. My team and I have been working super hard to find the killer of a woman who was murdered in her flat. She'd only been home from work less than an hour before her life was taken from her."

"No suspects at all?"

"We hauled the ex-boyfriend in within hours but were forced to release him. He's in the navy, based in Plymouth."

"Ouch. Would a serviceman really kill a civilian?"

"You'd be surprised, Dad. I've dealt with a few cases over the years that would prove your theory wrong. The good news is that before leaving work yesterday, I took a call from the pathologist dealing with the case, and she's stumbled across DNA she believes the killer left behind. Her team are searching the database for a possible match."

"I know what you're going to say. Without him being registered on the database through a previous crime, the likelihood of finding the killer is negligible."

Kayli nodded. "That's the frustrating part. I've told the team to take the day off and we'll hit the road running tomorrow. Maybe going over the evidence with fresh eyes will highlight something that we've missed up until now. I can't help wondering if my worrying about Mark has caused a distraction at work. I feel guilty for not getting the victim the justice she deserves."

"Nonsense. What utter tosh. How long has the case been open? A few days?"

Kayli nodded.

"Then how are you to blame for not solving it already? You know as well as I do that some cases take years to solve."

She shook her head. "Not on my patch, Dad. My team is one of the most competent in the Bristol area. We pride ourselves in solving the cases within a few weeks, max."

"Then stop worrying. You have another week and a half before you exceed your self-imposed deadline. Relax a little and start eating properly. That would be my advice. Mind you, your mother usually makes enough Sunday roast to feed a small army, so there's no fear of you going hungry today, lass."

They both laughed.

"Thanks for the pep talk, Dad."

He patted her on the knee. "You're always welcome. A problem shared and all that. Come on. I can smell that dinner isn't far off now. I better do my husbandly duty and lay the table or my life won't be worth living when you leave later. Of course, you're always welcome to stay with us for a little while, if you want to?"

"Thanks, I really appreciate the offer, Dad. It wouldn't feel right leaving the house unattended. I know it sounds daft, but when I'm at home, I can feel Mark around me."

"Doesn't sound silly at all. He'll be home soon enough, love. I guarantee it."

She hugged her father before they left his study. She spent the rest of the day with her parents, trying her hardest to put Mark's situation out of her mind. Her parents enveloped her with love as they relived special birthdays and days out during her childhood. She left their house at eight that evening, wearing a huge smile.

However, the second she stepped through the door of her home, the usual anxieties surfaced. After her head hit the pillow at ten o'clock, the same dream invaded her sleep.

She sat bolt upright at three o'clock in the morning, soaked in sweat. The more Kayli tried to shut off her thoughts, the more sleep evaded her. Finally, she gave in and went downstairs to make a cup of coffee. At five thirty, the house was pitch-black, and the wind was howling through a gap in the back door. She glanced out the window to see a mini-tornado in the rear garden. She shuddered and pulled her towelling robe tightly around her middle. Glancing up at the inky sky, she muttered, "Be safe, Mark. Come back to me soon. I miss you."

CHAPTER NINE

Kayli met Dave in the car park and rushed to help him get out of the car. "I bet you'll be glad to see the back of those crutches?"

"Morning. You could say that. It's the thought of climbing the stairs all the time that gets to me. Maybe we should put in a request to have a lift installed at the station. A bit archaic not to have one these days."

Kayli winked at him. "I'll have a word with the chief. Did you have a good day off?"

"Yeah, relaxing. I did bugger all except play with Luke all day."

"That sounds like heaven to me."

"You look tired. Have you slept at all? Or did you spend the day going out of your mind with worry?"

"The nights have been bad, waking up at three, but I went to Mum and Dad's yesterday and had a lovely day. It was good to get out of the house."

Dave locked the car and put his keys in his pocket, then they walked towards the entrance of the station. "I can't begin to image what you're going through at this tough time. Lord knows I keep trying to put myself in your shoes, but I just can't do it. You know we're all rooting for Mark, don't you?"

Kayli rubbed his arm. "I do, and it's really appreciated. Less chat—you need to channel your concentration into getting yourself up the stairs. I'll run on ahead and buy the coffees. That'll be an incentive for you." She laughed and raced ahead of her partner rather than listen to him grunting as he climbed the stairs on one good leg.

Dave barged through the door a few minutes later and flopped into his chair. "Christ, it feels like I've just climbed Mount Everest. It's getting harder every day instead of easier." He tapped his plaster at the ankle with his crutch. "Stupid leg, heal faster, will you?"

"It'll be off in a few weeks. I told you to take time off work, but no, you, being a martyr, were determined to continue to work."

He pulled a face at her. "I'm allowed to complain about my circumstances now and again."

Kayli laughed. "Okay, I'll give you that one."

Donna and Graeme arrived a few minutes later.

"I'll just flick through the post, see if anything needs my attention, then we'll crack on. Dave, can you chase up your tech guy for me first thing?"

"Already on my agenda to do it."

Kayli smiled and went into her office. She sat down at her desk just as her mobile rang. It was Giles. She hurriedly answered it, her breath catching in her throat. "Any news?"

"No. Sorry, sis. I was just ringing up to see how you are. Did you have fun yesterday?"

"Damn. I was hoping to hear something soon. Fun? Not exactly. I had a pleasant time with the folks, mostly reminiscing about what we got up to as kids."

"Sounds like fun to me. I'm going to do some chasing today. I'm concerned about Mark just as much as you are. I think things need to step up a gear over there before..."

"It's too late?" she said, finishing off his sentence.

"Yes. I'll do my best. Hopefully, I'll get back to you this afternoon or this evening with a plan of action."

"Sounds good to me. I know the guys out there are doing their best. They just need to do better."

"Sounds like you're writing a report on them." Giles chuckled.

"Sorry. Okay, keep me informed. I have to fly. Need to get my team set up with tasks for today."

"Okey-dokey, I'll call you later. Hopefully with some good news."

Distracted by her brother's call, Kayli decided to leave the mundane task of tearing open the post for another time and returned to her team.

"Anything, Dave?" she asked, approaching his desk as he was replacing his phone in its docking station.

"He's on it now. He asked me to give him a couple of hours, boss."

"Sounds fair enough to me. Let's go back over the details for the case in the meantime."

Dave's phone rang twenty minutes later. He beckoned Kayli over and placed the call on speaker. "Paddy, I've got you on speaker, so DI Bright can listen in on the conversation."

"Hello, Paddy. Any news for us?" Kayli asked.

"I have. I've managed to locate the phone through the GPS system."

Dave and Kayli stared at each other, their eyes wide open with excitement. "Go on, mate. Where is it?"

"Please don't tell me it's at the bottom of a river or something equally as bizarre as that?" Kayli said.

"No, I doubt if a signal would register if that were the case, ma'am," Paddy said.

"So?" Dave asked impatiently.

"It is kind of strange. I'm picking up a signal from the radio station in town."

Kayli groaned and slammed her fist against her thigh. "Damn, so she left the phone at work. Maybe it's in her desk or something. We should have asked the staff to check for us when we were there on Saturday."

"Can I interrupt you there, DI Bright?" Paddy asked.

"Sure, go ahead."

"Dave asked me to look at when the phone was last used. He also told me the victim's time of death and what time she arrived home from work. Piecing everything together, I can tell you that the victim placed a few calls *after* she arrived home."

"Are you sure, Paddy?" Dave asked.

"Positive. I'll send the details over to you."

Kayli cringed. "There's no need. We have the report. Damn, we concentrated on what numbers she'd called and not on the time the calls were made. We'll go over that again now. Thanks for your help, Paddy. Can you keep an eye on the phone's GPS for us and call us if it's on the move?"

"Straight away. Glad I could be of help. Good luck."

Dave hung up.

Kayli kicked out at the chair. "Shit! I'm screwing this case up."

Dave shook his head. "You're not. That kind of thing is easy to miss. Let's take another look at it now. Donna, do you have the list there?"

Donna left her seat and handed him the report. "I feel responsible. I should have spotted that too."

"Cut it out, guys. We'd just carried out a double shift. No one is to blame for missing what was right under our noses. Got that? We're a few days into the case, that's all. We would have stumbled across it eventually."

"Dave's right. There's no point dwelling on missed opportunities. We must make it a priority to right that wrong now. Let's study the list."

Dave's phone rang again. "Hello, DS Chaplin speaking... wait, just a second, Paddy. I'll put you on speaker again. Go ahead."

"Right. After I hung up, I managed to get a more accurate location for the phone. Stop blaming yourselves, guys, because the signal isn't coming from inside the building. It's coming from the car park, at least thirty feet away."

"Wow, you can do that?" Kayli asked.

"Pretty much. Just thought I'd let you know. Here's something else to consider. That phone must have been charged since her death. There's no way her battery would have lasted that long."

"Cheers, mate. That's brilliant news," Dave replied before hanging up.

Kayli held a finger up in the air, silencing everyone as she thought. "Donna, I need you to arrange search warrants for me. One for the radio station and one for all the cars sitting in the car park, to cover our backs."

Donna rushed back to her desk to make the call, and gave the thumbs-up to Kayli when the task had been actioned.

"Right, so looking at the list, Sarah rang two numbers after she arrived home. We need to try and trace those numbers. Dave, can you see if Paddy can do that for us rather than any of us ringing the numbers, just in case one of them belongs to the killer?"

Dave nodded and picked up the phone. Kayli's mouth dried up as the tension mounted. She headed for the vending machine and bought them all a cup of coffee. When she returned, Dave had a response for her.

"A Katrina Woodstock and a Tonya Burgen."

"Hmm... both female. Donna, can you look on Facebook, see if either of these ladies is on Sarah's friend list?"

Donna turned to her computer, and seconds later, she called back, "Bingo. They're both on her list as good friends and used to interact with her on most of her posts."

"Good news. Let's give them a ring. See what kind of mood Sarah was in leading up to her death. Ask the girls if she sounded strained at all during the conversation."

"Will do, boss."

Dave scratched his head. "What are you thinking? Regarding the cars at the radio station, I mean?"

"If Paddy is correct and the signal is coming from the car park, then I think Ryan has told some big fat lies. However, we need to trace that phone first before we start slinging accusations around. The only way we're going to do that is by getting the warrants. There's not a lot we can do before they come through."

"Did we carry out a background check on Ryan?" Dave asked, his brow furrowing a little.

"No, I don't think we did. Donna, can you do that for me please?"

Donna's hands flew across the keyboard, and within seconds, she was peering at her screen and jotting notes down on a sheet of paper. Intrigued, Kayli crossed the room and pulled up a chair alongside her. "No record as such, boss. Not on our system anyway. Only a couple of speeding notices. This is interesting, though. Looking at his employment record, he used to work at a well-known station in London before coming to Bristol."

"Why the move?"

"He was sacked for inappropriate behaviour with a colleague."

Kayli sat forward in her chair. "What? That's incredible. Why would another station even contemplate giving him a slot on their schedule, knowing what his reputation is like?"

"Seems strange to me, boss. Maybe he's popular and the person in charge at the station was willing to forget about his past in favour of high listener ratings," Donna suggested.

"I fear you're right. Morals clearly don't matter where business and ratings are concerned. Appalling... I wouldn't be able to live with myself if I employed someone like that. I doubt a woman would have opened the doors to him," Kayli said, lowering her voice to add the last part of her statement in case she upset the male members of her team.

"I think you're right," Donna agreed.

~ ~ ~

It was four hours before they were notified the warrants were ready. "I'm going to pick them up. Do you want to come with me, Dave?" Kayli called across the room.

He reached for his crutches and struggled to his feet. "You try and stop me. Want me to summon up some backup?"

"We'll sort it out with the desk sergeant on the way out. Wish us luck, guys."

"Good luck, boss," Graeme and Donna said in unison.

Kayli drove, her stomach twisting into knots during the journey.

"Do you think it best if we have a nosy around the cars first?" Dave asked.

With her eyes on the road ahead, Kayli nodded. "Yep, that's how I was going to play it. Do you want to stay in the car?"

"Nope. Two sets of eyes are better than one."

"Are you having a dig, Dave?"

He tutted, shaking his head. "No, and I wish you'd stop being so sensitive about things."

"Hard not to be when you come out with a comment like that, matey."

"Jeez... it was a harmless comment. I promise you I wasn't having a pop at you."

She grinned at him. "Good, because I'd hate for us to fall out about this."

"We won't, as long as you stop blaming yourself for slipping up."

"All right. It's done with now. I sure hope we find that phone. I can feel it in my water that something good is going to happen today."

"Umm... too much information there, boss, thanks. Maybe you're going to hear some good news about Mark rather than the case."

"I hope it's both. Giles is chasing up the team searching for him in Afghanistan. He said he'd ring me later with the results."

"That's good. I'm glad he's keeping you in the loop. You're lucky having him in your corner."

"I know. I love him to bits. We've always got on well together." She sighed heavily as she stopped at a red light. "Focus. I must focus on the job in hand, for now."

"You amaze me. You might doubt yourself at times, but I'm not sure I could switch off if Suranne was ever in trouble."

"I'm glad I have work to take my mind off things. Sitting at home stewing over the situation would drive me round the twist soon enough."

She entered the radio station's car park and drew the car to a halt at the far side, away from all the other cars. "I'm guessing the sports car is Ryan's. What do you think?"

"Umm... right. I suppose the personalised number plate was a hint."

Kayli chuckled. "I didn't even spot that. Hmm... DJ1012. Wonder if that's his date of birth."

"You're a scream. I wouldn't let him hear you say that. He seems the type to be defensive about divulging his real age."

"Okay, you start that side, and I'll begin over here."

They split up. She felt sorry for Dave having to hop between the cars, being extra careful not to touch the vehicles in case he set an alarm off. Kayli checked a few of the cars but didn't see anything obvious in either the back or the front of the vehicles. Next stop was Ryan's red Porsche—the status symbol for DJs, she presumed. The car was immaculate inside and out, as though it had recently been cleaned. *Damn, that's not good. There would be no evidence left behind if he's done that. Just our luck.*

Dave cleared his throat as she peered through the passenger window. She turned to face him. He beckoned her over with his head, without saying a word.

Kayli trotted across the car park with one eye on the entrance to the station. "Isn't this Danny Talbot's car?"

"It is indeed. Look under the front passenger seat. I can make out the end of a mobile."

She glanced through the window of the BMW and gasped. "It is. Whoa, hang on a second. We need to tread carefully here. It could be his mobile. Why don't we go inside and have a chat with him?"

"Exactly what I was going to suggest."

Kayli held open the heavy door for her partner to step into the station ahead of her. The receptionist looked up and smiled at them. "Hello again. Back so soon?"

"We are. We'd like a chat with Danny, if that's all right?"

"I'll call him and find out. I think they had a meeting planned for this afternoon. Not sure if that's finished or not yet."

"I'd appreciate it." Kayli swivelled and winked at her partner. "Keep your eyes open in case he makes a run for it."

"And you're expecting me to bring him down?"

"Ugh... okay, forget I mentioned it. Remind me why I asked you to tag along again?" she whispered.

"Because I'm the one who spotted the phone in the car," Dave said sarcastically.

"Touché. It would only have been a matter of time before I stumbled across it anyway."

A door along the corridor opened, and a group of people walked towards them. Leading the pack was Harry Jackson. "Hi, was there something else you needed, Detectives?"

"We'd like a chat with Danny if that's okay with you?"

He stepped aside and allowed Danny to come closer. "Hi, what can I do for you?"

"Do you mind if we have a quiet word in your office?" Kayli asked, smiling broadly.

"Not at all. This way."

He led them away from the group and into his office. He walked around the table, and before even taking a seat, he picked up his mobile to check if he had any missed calls or messages. Kayli glanced at Dave, adrenaline coursing rapidly through her veins.

"Take a seat. What's this about, Inspector? I told you everything I know the other day."

Kayli and Dave remained standing. "Maybe you wouldn't mind showing us the inside of your car?"

He frowned. "May I ask why?"

"Do you have something to hide, Mr. Talbot?" Dave challenged.

"Definitely not! Let me find my keys. They're around here somewhere." He lifted a few papers and moved things around on his desk.

"Try looking in your pocket," Dave suggested.

The young man patted down his trousers and tutted. "I'm such an idiot." His cheeks flared up with colour.

"Shall we?" Kayli motioned towards the door.

Talbot opened the door ahead of them and bolted out the room.

"Shit! I knew that would happen," Dave shouted.

Kayli was already on his tail. A few of Talbot's colleagues were still standing in the hallway. "Please, stop him!"

One person stood in the path of the absconding man and wrestled Danny to the ground. Ryan sat on his back until Kayli joined him. "Why are you running away from the nice police officer, toe rag? What have you got to hide?"

Kayli reached for her cuffs to slap them on one of Danny's wrists.

"Whoa! What is this?" Ryan asked a second time.

Danny bucked beneath Ryan. "Nothing. I ain't done nothing. This bitch has got nothing else to go on and is blaming..."

"Oh, don't stop there, Danny Boy. Let's all hear what you have to say. Why run if you've got nothing to hide?" Kayli asked.

Ryan stared at Kayli and pointed down at the man he was holding down beneath him. "Are you telling me he has something to do with Sarah's death?"

Kayli nodded. "We believe so."

"Why, you heap of horseshit." Ryan punched Danny several times in the head. "You were prepared to let one of us take the blame for what you did. Why?"

"Get off me, you tosser. I'll get my solicitor onto you," Danny growled, wriggling to get free.

Ryan punched him a couple more times before Dave arrived. "All right, Ryan, pack it in. We'll take it from here."

Ryan jumped to his feet, slapped the other cuff on Talbot's free wrist, and yanked Danny to his feet. "The worthless piece of shit is all yours, Inspector." Before he let go, he fisted Talbot in the stomach, causing him to double over.

Harry Jackson left a group of onlookers and demanded, "May I ask what the hell is going on here, Inspector?"

"You may. We have reason to believe that Danny has Sarah's phone in his vehicle. We had every intention of questioning him about it when his guilt surfaced, and he decided to make a run for it. That foolish gesture has pretty much sealed his fate."

"Is this true, Danny? Do you have Sarah's phone in your car?" Jackson asked his employee.

"I don't know. Perhaps she dropped it when I gave her a lift home."

"Maybe she did, but why run? Why not just say that in the first place? Or is it that you've had enough time to think up a plausible excuse?" Kayli asked.

"And he was pretty keen to let all of us take the heat from the police," Ryan said, surging forward to make contact with Talbot, except Dave stood in his way this time.

Dave warned him, "Leave it, man. He's not worth it. He'll get what's coming to him."

Kayli got hold of the cuffs and hoisted Talbot's arms high up his back, making him bend over slightly. "Thanks for all your help," she called over her shoulder at the bewildered onlookers. On the way out of the building, Kayli read the suspect his rights.

Dave removed Talbot's keys from his pocket, and once he was secured in the back seat of their car, Kayli and Dave made their way over to Talbot's car. Kayli pressed the key fob, and the doors clunked open. She pulled a plastic bag from her pocket and bent down to pick up the mobile phone that had led them to arrest Talbot. "We need to get SOCO here to pick up the vehicle," Kayli said, removing her mobile from her pocket to place the call.

Once that was arranged, they returned to the car and set off for the police station. Talbot sat in the back, a permanent scowl on his face, as if he were running through the events of the day Sarah was murdered.

Kayli refused to speak to him on the way to the station. She'd come up with the tactic early on in her career. Suspects were often infuriated by the silence, making them likely to slip up once they were in the interview room.

She pulled into the car park and went into the station. "Sergeant, do you have anyone free to help me in with a suspect? He's already tried to escape once, and what with Dave being incapacitated at present, I don't want to risk any more shenanigans."

"Of course. Salter, go with the inspector," he ordered a PC standing alongside him who was sorting through some paperwork.

The young officer quickly appeared at Kayli's side and followed her out to the car. Salter opened the back door, placed his hand on the man's head, and pulled Talbot's arm until he swung his legs round, easing himself out of the vehicle.

Kayli and Salter escorted the suspect into the station while Dave hoisted himself out of the car.

"This is Danny Talbot. He's been arrested for the murder of Sarah Abel, if you can process him for me, Sergeant. I need his DNA to be sent to Forensics as soon as you can. I'll interview him when I have the time. Make him comfortable in a cell until then, if you would?"

"Will do, ma'am. Do you want me to call a duty solicitor for you?"

"Yes, leave it an hour or so. I have a few things to sort out first." Kayli glanced at Talbot, whose chin was resting on his chest. He was obviously feeling sorry for himself. She shook her head in disgust and walked up the stairs.

Donna and Graeme turned to look at her, eager to hear the news. Kayli punched the air. "We've got him. Dave spotted the mobile poking out from underneath the passenger seat. He tried to run as soon as we told him we wanted to inspect his car." She held up the bag with the phone inside. "Donna, I need you to get me a warrant for Talbot's address ASAP."

"Consider it done, boss. Congratulations."

Dave came into the room and rushed towards his chair. "Blimey, I swear those stairs are getting steeper every time I walk up them."

They all laughed at the sweat forming on his brow. "I think we could all do with a coffee." Kayli bought and distributed the drinks. She took her coffee into the office and sat down at her desk. After taking a couple of sips, she picked up the phone on her desk and placed a call.

"Hi, Naomi. It's Kayli. I have good news for you."

"We won the lottery in the syndicate, and they chose you to break the news to us all?"

Kayli laughed and relaxed into her chair. "Nope, not this time. I had no idea you played in a syndicate."

"There's a lot you don't know about me, Inspector. Are you going to share this good news with me, or keep me dangling?"

"We've arrested someone for Sarah Abel's murder. I've called SOCO to pick up the suspect's car, and I'm awaiting a warrant to search his address."

"Excellent news. I'm delighted for you. Are you going to tell me who it is?"

"The man who gave her a lift home that night after work."

"Whoa! A work colleague? Any idea why?"

"Not yet. I want to see what's in his flat first before I tackle him. He's a butter-wouldn't-melt kind of guy. Sickening that he would take her life the way he did. My take is that he doubled back to see her after saying farewell. We know he drove off, or we suspect he did as the boyfriend witnessed him leave. Actually, Young said he drove away after he saw her kiss him."

"Either way, you've got him. May I ask how?"

"We managed to trace her phone via the GPS to his vehicle."

"I'm not with you. Did she drop it in his car? That's hardly condemning evidence, Kayli."

Kayli sighed and smiled at the same time. "It wouldn't be ordinarily, but we have proof that she made a couple of calls from home, spoke to two friends whilst inside her flat. There's no way she could have done that if she'd left the phone in Talbot's car."

"Great detective work. Well done. Let me know when you get the warrant. I'll put a team on standby for you."

"Excellent. Thanks, Naomi. I'll speak to you soon."

They had a long wait before the warrant was issued. The time was almost five o'clock. "Great, another late night," Kayli announced to the team. "Donna, do me a favour and ring the pathologist. She's awaiting my call. I want to get over to the address before it gets too late. Graeme, Dave, I want you to come with me."

"I'll take my car, boss," Graeme replied, standing up to slip on his jacket.

"I was going to suggest the same. Are you up to this, Dave?"

Dave nodded emphatically. "Yep, the adrenaline is kicking in, giving me my second wind."

~ ~ ~

When the three of them arrived at Talbot's flat in the centre of the city, they found a shabby exterior but a very neat interior. The place was a typical bachelor pad. Everything was either grey, white or black—no splashes of bright colour. The lack of pictures and knickknacks made it obvious that a woman had never resided in the flat. Kayli and her team, wearing the obligatory plastic gloves, began to search the flat. It didn't take them long to find the evidence they were seeking.

Kayli pushed open the door to the bedroom and gasped. Shaking her head in disgust, she entered the room. Every conceivable inch of wall space was taken up with photos of the victim. The man was clearly besotted with Sarah, and Kayli couldn't help wondering if Sarah knew.

Dave whistled. "Jesus, he's one sick fucker."

Graeme opened a wardrobe door and reeled. "Bloody hell, what a stench." Kayli placed a hand over her nose and mouth and joined him. She knelt down to rummage through the items at the bottom and extracted a light-brown jumper that had evidence of vomit on it. Beside it was a black balaclava. "Crap, I bet this belongs to Sarah."

"What? The jumper or the vomit?" Dave asked, shaking his head.

"My guess is the latter."

Kayli heard voices in the front room, and Graeme went to see who it was.

"The forensic team has arrived," Graeme said, poking his head back in.

"Good, let's get them in here to bag this lot up."

Two forensic guys walked in and looked around them. "Okay, do you want to leave this to us now, Inspector? Is there anything specific you're looking for?" the younger guy asked.

Kayli held out the jumper. "I think everything we need is on this. Plus, his infatuation of the victim is evident on the walls."

"Don't worry. We'll photograph it all for you and get the DNA results back to you ASAP."

"Brilliant. We'll leave you to it then and call it a day."

Kayli, Dave, and Graeme left the room.

Dave shook his head, surprised. "Really? You're going home now? What about Talbot's interview?"

"Yes, I've made the decision to let him rot in a cell overnight. I'll interview him first thing in the morning. We've got enough on him now not to be concerned about him getting away with this."

"Your call. I'm not objecting. My leg is giving me jip anyway, so I could do with an early night."

"Why don't I drop you home? You can get a taxi into work in the morning. How does that sound?"

"Sounds good to me, if you don't mind?"

"It's not as if I'm doing anything else tonight."

The three of them left the house and went their separate ways. When she dropped Dave off at home, he tried his hardest to persuade her to join him and Suranne for something to eat, but Kayli rejected the offer. "All I want to do is go home and soak in the bath, matey, but I appreciate the offer. Have a good evening."

"You too. Glad we nailed the bastard today."

"Me too. We're still the best team around."

CHAPTER TEN

Kayli drove into work the next day, still buoyed about arresting Talbot, but regretting that she'd lain awake most of the night, thinking about Mark.

The team were all laughing when she entered the incident room. "Glad to see spirits are so high. We need to sort out a celebratory drink. How about tonight?"

"Sounds good to me," Dave was the first to reply. Graeme and Donna followed suit.

"That's sorted then. Right, Dave, are you going to join me for the interview? The desk sergeant has placed the call for the duty solicitor to join us."

"Try and keep me away."

They left the office ten minutes later. Talbot entered the interview room, his hair a mess, and he had dark circles around his eyes, hinting at his lack of sleep. The duty solicitor was a young man Kayli had seen once or twice before by the name of Abbott.

Dave initiated the tape recording and announced who was in the room before Kayli hit Talbot with her first question. "Why? Why did you kill Sarah Abel, Mr. Talbot?"

His head sank onto his chest. "I didn't mean to."

"What do you mean? Are you telling us that you were in her flat the day she died?"

He nodded. "Yes. I went back to ask her a question."

"After you dropped her off, you're telling me you entered her flat?" Kayli asked, clarifying what the suspect said.

"That's right."

Kayli twisted her pen in her right hand. "What question did you expect her to answer?"

"I wanted to know if she wanted to go to a concert with me at the weekend."

"I see. And what was her reaction to that?"

"Things didn't go to plan. She'd already rejected me once, it made my blood boil. I rang the bell and hid. She was just about to close the door, something inside snapped. I barged into the house."

"And what happened then?"

"I tied her up in the bedroom. You know the rest," he added brusquely.

"You killed her. Someone you were so infatuated with. Why? Because she rejected you, or was there more to it than that?"

He was silent for a few moments then raised his head to look at her, a smirk pulling at his mouth. "She got what she deserved. She could have had it all with me, but she chose to deny her feelings for me. She flirted with me every second of the day at work."

Kayli's eyes narrowed. "She kissed you on the cheek goodbye. That was what triggered all this, wasn't it? You thought she was giving you the come-on and knocked on her door, hoping she would let you into her bed. How am I doing?"

Glaring at her, he shrugged.

"Instead, she rejected your advances. If you loved her that much, why did you set out to kill her? There's no point denying how deep your feelings were for her—we've seen her pictures plastered over your bedroom walls at your flat."

"We could have been happy together. Even when she realised her life was about to end, she took pleasure in rejecting me. Told me that she was going to get back with him."

"Him? Young, you mean?"

"Yes. She was too good for him."

"And for you apparently," Kayli snapped back harshly. "I've heard enough. To me, you've confessed to murdering Sarah Abel. Is there anything else you'd like to tell us before I end this interview?"

"Nope. I'd do it all over again, given the opportunity. She was a tease, loved flaunting her flesh at work."

"In your eyes only, it would appear. Over the course of our investigation, we've heard nothing but good things about Sarah. Maybe you imagined her to be something she clearly wasn't. Mislabelled her to suit your needs, and when she rejected you... well, we all know what your reaction to that was, don't we?"

He hung his head in shame at last.

Kayli shook her head. "You'll be formerly charged and sent to a detention centre by the end of the day."

Dave ended the tape, and Kayli motioned for the PC to escort the suspect from the room.

"Thanks for coming, Mr. Abbott."

"My pleasure." The solicitor shook her hand.

Kayli and Dave left the room with the solicitor, who went through to the reception area while they walked slowly up the stairs again. When they reached the top, Kayli's mobile rang. Her brother's name filled the small screen. "Hello, you. What can I do for you?"

"You sound happy?" Giles noted.

She detected a little tension in his voice. "Unlike you. What's wrong? It's not Annabelle, is it?"

"No, love. Everyone is fine here. Are you sitting down?"

Kayli leaned against the bannister and looked over at Dave.

He rubbed her arm and mouthed, "Are you okay?"

She nodded and swallowed. A vice-like grip clenched her heart. "Go on. I'm sitting," she lied.

"Kayli... they've spotted him."

Her legs gave way beneath her. Dave tried to break her fall, but his crutches got in the way. Tears swiftly filled her eyes. "Where? When?"

"In Kabul. Intel says that he was being moved someplace else."

"Where to?" She tried to stand, but her legs gave way again.

"That's the thing—we don't know. Listen, that's not important. At least we know he's alive now."

"My God, I don't believe it. What now?"

"We sit and wait."

"What? No way!" She looked up at Dave as she said, "I'm going out there."

"You are *not!*" Giles shouted as Dave shook his head.

"Watch me," she said defiantly. Forcing her legs to work, she stood up. "We've just wrapped up the case. I'm going to see the DCI now. Get me on a plane, Giles. I don't care if it's on its last legs. Just get me on a plane."

"You're crazy. I can't—no, I won't let you go out there alone."

She gasped. "Then come with me."

"What? I can't do that. What about Annabelle?"

"Sorry, I was being selfish. Get in touch with your contacts and tell them to expect me soon, Giles. I'm deadly serious about this."

"I know you are. Jesus, you can be such a stubborn bitch at times, sis. Give me a couple of hours to sort things out. Oh fuck! Mum and Dad are going to kill me when they hear about this."

"They won't. They'll understand." Kayli hung up and stared at her partner, whose mouth gaped open. She shrugged. "I have to do this, Dave."

"I know. You know what? If I were in your situation, I'd be saying exactly the same thing. I can't believe I'm saying this, but you better go and clear it with the DCI."

"Wish me luck." She raced along the corridor and into Fiona's office. "Sorry, it's an emergency. I need to see her now."

"Let me make the call," Fiona replied, frowning. She swiftly picked up the phone. "DCI Davis, I have Inspector Bright here needing to see you urgently... Okay, I'll send her in."

Kayli smiled, and before the secretary could hang up the phone, she knocked on the door and entered the DCI's inner sanctum.

DCI Davis was sitting upright in her chair, a pile of paperwork on the desk in front of her. "Is something wrong, Inspector?"

"Two things I needed to see you about, ma'am. I think I'll need to sit down before I tell you, if that's okay?"

DCI Davis placed her pen on top of the papers she was dealing with and pushed them to one side. "This looks serious. You better get to the point, Inspector. Do you have a problem with the case, or is this personal?"

She sighed and smiled half-heartedly. "You'll be pleased to know that we've just arrested a suspect for the murder of Sarah Abel."

"I see. Therefore, this visit must be personal." She sat back in her chair and clenched her hands together in front of her."

Kayli's gaze drifted to the bookshelves behind the chief, and she struggled to keep the tears from forming. She gulped and inhaled a shuddering breath. "I need time off, ma'am."

"Of course. I thought you were struggling to cope. It must be hard with Mark missing. Glad you managed to bring the case to a satisfactory conclusion. I appreciate all the effort you put in on this case."

"I was only doing my job, ma'am. Giles, my brother, rang me a few moments ago to inform me that Mark has been spotted in Afghanistan."

DCI Davis sat upright and bounced forward in her chair. "That's great news, isn't it? Why the glum face?"

"Because he's still a prisoner. He was in the process of being moved, and we have no idea where to. All I know is that he needs me. I can't tell you more than that, but I need to go out there and rescue him."

The DCI's eyes widened. "Are you serious? You can't go out there. It's far too dangerous for you. For any civilian woman, come to that. Please reconsider your decision."

Kayli shook her head defiantly. "I won't do that. My mind is made up. I'm going. My brother is making all the arrangements now. I just needed to clear things with you first. Look, I'll understand if you think I'm running out on you and you need to fill my shoes, especially when Dave is incapacitated at present, but my need to help rescue Mark far outweighs my desire to chase criminals at the moment. It's imperative that I do this, and I'm hoping you'll understand my reasons why."

DCI Davis threw her hands up in the air and left her chair. She walked around her desk and perched her backside on it ahead of Kayli. She took Kayli's hand in her own. "No one truly understands the power of love until they're faced with an impossible situation such as this. I will not stand in your way, and to be brutally honest with you, if I were in your shoes, I'd stubbornly be saying the same thing. Answer me this, though? Have you *truly* considered the danger you'll be putting yourself through?"

Kayli nodded. "I know what my life has been like over the past few weeks and how intolerable it has been sleeping in my bed alone. I love him. If there's a way for me and Giles to get him back, then I'm willing to risk everything to do that."

"But we're talking about being interred in a different culture, where women are treated as second-class citizens the majority of the time. What makes you think you can just roll up in this God-forsaken country and extract your fiancé?"

"I hear what you're saying, boss. I haven't taken the decision lightly, I swear. You know as well as I do that I'm no ordinary woman. I have balls bigger than most men I know." Kayli sniggered, trying to ease the tension that had built up in the room. She ran a hand over her face and brushed a stray hair behind her ear.

"I know determination when I see it. I also recognise that I'd be wasting my time trying to persuade you to reconsider. I'm on the fence about this one. I desperately want you to stay for selfish reasons and for your own safety. However, I totally understand your desire to be the one to rescue Mark. I wouldn't be doing my job if I didn't try and dissuade you, though, right?"

"I know. Believe me, if the tables were turned, I'd be saying exactly the same thing to you, ma'am. If I hadn't been having these vivid dreams lately, I probably wouldn't be considering taking the trip." She placed her flattened hand over her heart and wiped away a stray tear with her other hand. "The pain here is too strong to deny. If I fail, at least I'll know that I tried my very best for him. I won't get that satisfaction staying around here."

"But we're talking about *Afghanistan* here, not the South of France."

Kayli smiled and tried to remove her hand from the chief's, but her boss held firm. "I know. The dangers will probably overwhelm me once I land in the country. All I know is that it wouldn't be right for me to stay here when Mark needs me so badly."

"Tell me about your dreams."

Kayli shook her head. "I can't. It's too personal, ma'am."

"Nonsense. I'm ordering you to tell me. Come on."

Kayli's head dropped to her chest. "I see him in chains, wasting away. He looks up at me and tells me they're starving him to death. My heart leapt when Giles told me he'd been spotted. My hopes have been raised that he's still alive. I should be satisfied with the news, but if anything, it's made me even more determined to go out there. I'm not saying that it will be a successful mission, but in my heart and in my head, I'll have the satisfaction of knowing that I did all I could to help save him."

"I truly understand. Come here." DCI Davis stood up and pulled Kayli into her arms. At first, Kayli stiffened, objecting to the DCI's sudden bout of soppiness, but then she relaxed into her arms and found herself sobbing for the next few minutes. Davis held her at arm's-length and wiped away Kayli's tears, her own eyes welling up with emotion. "I won't stand in your way, and I willingly give you my blessing. I'll sanction two weeks of emergency holiday time for you. Do you think that will be enough?"

Nodding, Kayli sniffed, and the DCI handed her a tissue from the box sitting on her desk. "I think so. Can I have the option to extend if I need to?"

"Of course. Now go, bring that wonderful man of yours home. I need to see the smile on your face again around here."

"Gosh, I haven't been that bad, have I?"

"No comment. Most of all, take care of yourself. Don't take unnecessary risks, and for Christ's sake, don't get caught. I dread to think what those animals are likely to do with you if you are."

Kayli laughed and shook her head. "Oh shit! Thanks for that, boss. Very reassuring words to take with me."

DCI Davis waved a hand in front of her. "Get out of here. You know what I mean. Hey, great news on solving the murder case. I had every faith in you doing that even with your mind not always on the job."

"You caught that, did you? Dave put me on the straight and narrow a few times. The team is in safe hands in my absence."

"I know that. I'll bring him in later, read him the riot act."

Kayli's mouth dropped open.

"Where's your sense of humour gone? I'll run through a few things with him, make sure he knows I'm here if he needs me, not that that kind of thing ever works with you."

"Nonsense. I always rely on you to back me up, or when I have a problem that needs solving."

"Hmm... sometimes. Go on. Get yourself off. Stay safe, and if at all possible, ring me when you can."

"I promise. Thank you, boss, from the bottom of my heart. I truly appreciate you backing me like this."

"I know. I wouldn't do it if you were a shitty inspector."

Kayli leaned forward and shared another hug with DCI Davis before rushing out the room.

She inhaled a large breath and entered the incident room. Three anxious gazes all looked her way.

"The DCI has sanctioned my time off. I have two weeks to rescue Mark and return home."

"Oh right, you think it's going to be that simple, Kayli?" Dave said, folding his arms across his tight chest.

She smiled and walked towards him. "Have faith in my abilities, partner. You're in charge until I get back. The chief will want a word with you today. Don't be worried about that. She's a pussycat, really."

Dave groaned and rolled his eyes. "Thanks, that's something to look forward to—*not*. When are you setting off?"

"Giles is busy making all the arrangements. I'm going to shoot home now and do some packing."

"Do you know what to pack? What kind of weather are they having out there at the moment, boss?" Donna asked.

Kayli tutted. "Crap, I have no idea."

Donna raised a finger and turned to her computer. Within seconds, she had traced the regional weather forecast for Afghanistan via Google. "It's pretty variable. Anything between fifteen and twenty-five degrees during the day. However, it can drop below zero at night."

"Thanks, Donna. I suppose I better pack a bikini or two and a few jumpers too."

Dave's jaw dropped. "You can't frigging do that. No matter how hot it gets out there, you're going to have to keep yourself covered. You start flashing creamy-white skin around..."

Kayli laughed. "Christ, when did you become so gullible? Of course I won't be exposing my skin over there. I'd hate to end up with sunstroke."

Dave shrugged and shook his head. "Now I know you're winding me up."

She winked at him. "I'm going. Be good. And don't fret about me—that's an order. You guys know how resilient I am."

"Let's hope you can remember some of your martial art skills," Dave replied.

"Don't worry. That's not something you tend to forget when you're up against things. Be good, chaps and chapess."

She quickly hugged each member of her team and ran out of the room before they could witness her breaking down again.

When she arrived home, she flew up the stairs, pulled out a small suitcase, and began throwing her underwear inside while she thought about what other clothes to take. She decided she would be better off taking darker clothes and settled on three pairs of leggings and set aside a pair of skin-tight black jeans for the journey. Four heavy jumpers and five T-shirts were slotted into the case along with two sets of trainers, a pair of ankle boots, and a nightshirt. Kayli rushed into the bathroom and packed her toothbrush and toothpaste into her toiletry bag.

Next Kayli returned downstairs and opened a can of soup, aware that she should be eating something more substantial in the likelihood that she and Giles would be leaving soon, but her stomach was too knotted to consider eating anything else.

At eight thirty, she was pacing the floor, when Giles called her mobile. "Be at my house for six in the morning."

"Really? We're going tomorrow?"

"Yep, all the details have been finalised. Don't forget your passport, love." His voice lowered. "Thanks to you, I'm in the doghouse here."

"Shit! Sorry. You stay here, and I'll go by myself then. The last thing I want is for Annabelle to fall out with me."

"No chance. I'm coming with you. Umm... I think you better forewarn Mum and Dad."

Kayli sucked in air and blew out a breath. "I'll do it now before I go to bed. Thanks for this, Giles. You'll never know how much this means to me."

"I think I can hazard a guess. See you in the morning. Sweet dreams."

Kayli hung up and immediately dialled her parents' number. Her mother answered the phone right away. "Hi, Mum. How are you?"

"Can't complain, lovely. We've had to resort to putting the central heating on tonight, a sure sign that winter is rearing its ugly head. How's the case going?"

"All solved, Mum. The culprit is tucked up in a cell at the station until he can be moved to a detention centre tomorrow."

"Excellent news. Was it the ex-boyfriend?"

"Nope. It was a colleague of the victim. Shameful really. He gave her a lift home from work that evening and doubled back to see her. That's when the deed was done. Look, I have something to tell you and Dad. Is he there? Can you put the phone on speaker, so I can tell you both at the same time?"

"Oh gosh! You're not pregnant like Annabelle, are you?"

Kayli laughed. "Give me some credit, Mum. No, I'm not about to deliver you your third grandchild."

"That's a shame, dear. Hold on a moment. I'll give your father a shout. He'll have to put this contraption on speaker. I'm hopeless at doing that, always tend to cut people off." The phone clattered on a hard surface, then she heard her mother calling her father. He chuntered on about being busy until Kayli's mother told him she was on the phone, wanting to speak to them both.

"You're on speaker now, darling. How are you?" her father asked.

"Hi, Dad. I wanted to tell you both together." She paused and cleared her throat to dislodge the sudden lump that had formed. "Giles and I are going on a trip tomorrow. He asked me to pass on the news."

"How exciting. Are you all going on holiday? With Annabelle and Bobby?" her mother asked.

"Hmm... I'm not getting that impression, Moira. Let the child speak," her father silenced his wife abruptly.

Kayli closed her eyes, and before she realised she'd even opened her mouth, she told them, "No. It's not a holiday as such. We're travelling out to Afghanistan on a rescue mission." Her eyes remained tightly closed as she waited for the onslaught from her parents.

Her mother gasped and broke down in tears. That was all Kayli could hear until her father said, "I think you're being bloody foolish, Kayli. You both are."

"I'm sorry you think that, Dad. I have to go. Mark needs me."

"What utter tosh that is. He needs you to be here for him for when he returns home. Not out there, risking your life, as well as your brother's. What does Annabelle have to say about this?"

"Giles just called to say he's in the doghouse. Why aren't you all prepared to back us on this one? I'll be with Giles. I'm not aware of the finer details of the rescue plan yet. However, I'm presuming that Giles has a military team out there willing to give us some backup if we need it."

"But you don't know that for a fact. Kayli, you have no idea what savages these people are. What will likely happen to you if you fall into the hands of either the Taliban or, worse still, ISIS. They behead people just for the sake of it and rape all the women and children without a second thought. That's their own people, by the way. I dread to think how they would treat a Western woman. Bloody hell, this is insane. I can't believe you and your brother can be so selfish. To have no thoughts for your mother and me—or Annabelle and Bobby! It's absurd, I tell you. I'm bloody furious about this."

Kayli ran a shaking hand over her face. Over the years, her father had never raised his voice at her. She was at a loss for words.

"Are you still there, Kayli?" her father shouted.

"I'm here. Please, Dad, don't be angry with me. It's your support Giles and I need, not your anger. Mum, what do you think?"

Her mother sniffled and whispered, "I'm with your father on this one, dear. Please, let the men more suited to tasks like this deal with it over there. You have no awareness of what awaits you."

"Exactly. Kayli, you're being unreasonable about this, and I'm begging you to reconsider your decision."

Kayli felt torn. Her desire to rescue Mark far outweighed her need to appease her parents. They were wrong about one thing: she was totally aware of the dangers ahead of her. "Mum, Dad, I love you dearly. The last thing I want or need right now is to fall out with you both, but my mind is made up. I'm sorry. I have to go now. I need to finish packing before I go to bed. Lord knows if I'll be able to sleep or not. I love you both. Please remember that. Also remember that I haven't taken this decision lightly. Mark needs me—needs us—to help him. Love you both. Nothing will ever change that." Kayli hung up before either of her parents could speak again.

The phone rang constantly for the rest of the evening. Kayli ignored it, knowing that it would be her parents, trying their best to dissuade her from going. She felt bad, but no one was going to be able to do that. Once she was adamant about something, no matter how dangerous, she always saw that notion through to its conclusion. Rescuing Mark was the only thing that mattered to her now. The phone finally went silent around nine thirty.

She went to bed and lay awake for several hours, her thoughts filled with what she was likely to find out in Afghanistan. That was when the stark reality hit her. *What if the mission fails? What if we're too late and Mark is already dead? What if these monsters abduct me? What if I never return? What will happen to this place? I should have put a will in place by now. What am I thinking, going over there at the drop of a hat?* The same questions were repeated over and over again as she searched for the answers. It was gone three before she finally drifted off to sleep.

CHAPTER ELEVEN

Kayli was too nervous to even consider having breakfast that morning. Instead, she set off for Giles's house at five thirty and was standing on his doorstep a mere fifteen minutes later. He greeted her at the door, looking as tired as she felt. He placed a finger to his lips and invited her in.

"I told Annabelle to stay in bed," Giles said, kissing her on the cheek.

Kayli placed her suitcase at the bottom of the stairs. "Is she still mad at you?"

"You could say that." Giles pointed to her suitcase. "What's that?"

She chuckled. "What does it look like?"

He shook his head and gave her a stern look. "You can't take that, love. It's got to be the bare minimum. We're not going on holiday."

"I realise that, and believe me, that is the bare minimum."

He bent down and unzipped the case then collected his kitbag, which was sitting a few feet away, and opened it. Kayli watched as he sifted through her suitcase and rammed what he considered to be essentials into his own bag before he closed his kitbag again. "That should do you. Are you ready to go? Do you have your passport?"

She opened her small handbag and extracted her passport. "I have."

"Good. I'll allow you to take your purse and your passport. Your handbag will have to remain here."

"Crap, Giles, seriously?"

"I'm deadly serious."

The stairs creaked as Annabelle descended. Her terrified glance swept between them. "I can't believe you're both going." She raised her hand to prevent either of them from speaking. "But I couldn't let you go without saying goodbye. Please, whatever happens out there, promise me you'll think with both your heart *and* your head. Most of all, come back to us, unharmed. We love you both. I might not agree with what you're doing, but that doesn't stop me caring about what happens to you both. Stick together at all times."

Kayli rushed into her arms. "I'm sorry for dragging Giles into this. I need to help Mark, though. You understand that, right?"

"I do. I'm still angry with you both. However, I didn't want you going over there distracted. I'll cope with my anger in your absence and will be sending positive thoughts to you throughout your mission. Look after each other. You're all I've got." She ran a hand over the tiny bump that had developed in the last week or so. "This one needs you guys."

Giles kissed Annabelle and hugged her tightly. "I have every intention of returning in one piece. I'll do my darnedest to ensure all three of us return safely, and quickly. We'll be in touch when we can, love, I promise you. Take care of yourself and Bobby in the meantime."

"I will. Shouldn't you be going? What time is your flight?"

"At nine fifteen. You're right. We should be getting a move on." Giles picked up his kitbag and hoisted the strap over his shoulder.

Kayli glanced down at her suitcase. "He says I can't take that. Shall I put it upstairs in the spare room?"

"No, you go. I'll deal with that." Annabelle squeezed her. "Stay safe. I hope you find Mark soon, sweetie."

Kayli pulled away, her eyes moist with tears. "Me too, and once again, I'm sorry for getting Giles involved in this mission."

Annabelle smiled and looked over at her husband. "I think you'd have had a devil of a job preventing him from getting involved. Just be safe, the pair of you. Touch base when you can. I'll be sure to pass on any news I have to your parents."

Kayli's head dropped, ashamed at the way she'd treated her parents the evening before. "We had words last night. I hung up on them, and they kept ringing me all night, but I refused to answer. I'm not sure they'll ever understand my reasons for going over there, but will you tell them how much I love them when you speak to them later?"

"Of course I will, not that they don't realise that already, love. They're just concerned about you—we all are."

"Come on, Kayli. We need to go." Giles tugged on her arm.

"Tell them I love them no matter what they think of me," Kayli said, following her brother out the front door.

"I will. Be safe, guys. I love you both."

Giles opened the boot of the car, threw his kitbag in, and slammed the door shut. Then he bolted back to the house and kissed Annabelle again. Giles looked emotional as he slid behind the steering wheel of his car. Guilt rested heavily on Kayli's shoulders during the silent journey to the airport.

Once they'd parked the car in the car park, they booked Giles's kitbag in for the flight then went in search of a café.

"I'm in dire need of caffeine. Do you want anything to eat?" Kayli asked, her eyes glazing over at the scrummy pastries on display, tempting the customers.

"I'm fine. You have something if you want to."

Kayli chose an apricot Danish and offered a section of it to her brother once they were sat at the table.

He politely refused, and his gaze drifted out the large window, at the aeroplanes being prepared for take-off.

"What's the plan when we get to Turkey?" she asked.

"We have to travel to a military base and board a plane that will take us to Kabul Airport. From there, we'll get a chopper to Kandahar. That's where we're going to meet up with the rest of the team."

"This team, who are they exactly?"

"A mixture of the security team I used to work for and a covert military team that are operating in that area."

"That's brilliant news. Now we're on our way and that you no longer work for the security firm, can you tell me what the job entailed?"

"I guess I can now. We were employed to drive heads of a Chinese gemstone company working in the area. Most people think that oil is big business over there—it isn't. That's what the Iraq War was predominantly about, although the US and UK governments will always deny that fact and use the weapons-of-mass-destruction excuse until the cows come home."

"Very sad. I had no idea Afghanistan is rich in gemstones. Why would they need protecting?"

Giles raised his eyebrows. "Neither did Mark and I, until we set foot in the country. Afghanistan is rich in not only gemstones, but minerals too. Of course they still dabble in growing thousands of acres of poppies to supply the heroin trade."

"I bet most of that shit ends up on the streets of the UK, right?"

Giles nodded. "Unfortunately, yes. Going back to the gemstone aspect, things are a tad antsy between the Chinese and the Taliban. I have no idea at this point why they abducted Mark. I can only presume that they've kidnapped one of the directors of the gemstone company at the same time. We won't know until we get out there."

"But things usually end peacefully? It's all about money at the end of the day, isn't it? The Taliban wouldn't kill the Chinese representatives if they knew they could exploit cash from them, right?"

"You're spot on. They're probably holding the Chinese director in a hotel somewhere and taking their anguish out on Mark to possibly twist their arms into doing something. What that is, we'll probably never find out."

"Why does everything have to be about money all the time? What are we going into? Has the country been rebuilt now?"

He shook his head and took a sip of his coffee. "You have a rude awakening coming your way if you think the country is up and running again after the war. Our team was of the opinion that it's more of a warzone now than it ever was."

"I had no idea. I wish either you or Mark had confided in me, instead of keeping me in the dark."

"What's done is done, sis. You'll see what things are like out there for yourself soon enough."

They boarded the plane at eight fifteen. Kayli was already regretting eating the pastry as her stomach constricted while they awaited take-off. She was surprised how full the plane was, given the time of year.

~ ~ ~

Six hours later, long after Kayli had grown bored with staring out the window, the plane touched down in Ankara. They collected Giles's kitbag and hopped in a taxi, which drove them to the military airbase a few miles away, where they would embark on the second leg of their long journey. Giles seemed agitated. Therefore, Kayli kept any questions she was dying to ask under wraps.

They arrived at the military base and were swiftly transported by jeep to a terminal to await their second flight. This was a totally different setup to the commercial airport. The café, which was more like a spit-and-sawdust canteen, offered only tea or coffee in plastic cups.

Finally, a young man in army uniform arrived to escort them out to the tarmac.

"Thanks for your help," Giles said, shaking the young man's hand before they boarded the small plane.

As soon as they entered the plane, Kayli felt claustrophobic. Her fear of confined spaces took over all her senses. Her palms became sweaty instantly, and her brow broke out in droplets of moisture as she felt her cheeks flare up with heat.

Once seated, Giles turned to look at her. "Jesus, I forgot. Are you all right?"

Kayli held back, refusing to break down in tears, and nodded. "I'm going to have to be. How long is the flight?"

"Five hours, give or take a few minutes. Stick with it, love. Will it help if you have a sleep?"

"I'm too frigging scared to close my eyes. Shit, I didn't feel this bad on the other plane."

Giles chuckled. "A stark contrast in size and comfort. Maybe you should imagine yourself on a commercial flight."

"I can try. God, I feel like shit."

"I hate to remind you, but we have a helicopter ride to contend with after this one."

Her body started to tremble at the thought. "What the hell am I doing here?"

Giles reached for her hand and grasped it between both of his. "Look at it this way: this adventure will either kill you or cure your phobia."

Kayli stared at him. "And you think that is going to make me feel better?"

He shrugged. "Just close your eyes and try to relax. The journey will be over before you know it."

"Your logic is so off-the-wall sometimes, brother dearest. I have five hours to endure. It would be different if my punishment consisted of being trapped in this tin can for half an hour."

"It's hardly a tin can. I think you're over-exaggerating there, sis."

Not long after, the plane began to taxi up the runway. It was far noisier than any commercial flight she'd taken, and before long, she had a headache to go along with her other symptoms.

She exhaled a large breath when the plane finally started on its final descent. Kayli glanced out of the window at the terrain and saw very little on the approach except for desert. But as they got closer to their destination, a large town with numerous buildings, large and small, appeared below them.

"Not long now. You're doing exceptionally well, sis."

Kayli smiled and gripped her brother's hand as the plane grew noisier. "I'll be fine once I can feel the ground beneath my feet."

"It won't be for long, love. We'll be whisked away and thrown into the chopper virtually straight away."

"Did you have to tell me that?" She winced as the wheels touched down on the tarmac. The plane bounced a few times before it glided to a halt. Kayli exhaled a large breath as the door swung open and fresh air filled the cabin.

Giles brushed a hand over her cheek. "Night will be setting in soon. Are you ready for the final part of our journey?"

"As I'll ever be. If I waited around to think things over, I doubt I'd volunteer to take the trip tonight. It's been a long day so far."

"The sooner we get there, the better, love. Dig deep."

Kayli nodded and followed her brother off the aircraft, smiling at the attendant who had opened the door.

Giles pointed at the helicopter sitting on the tarmac. "Looks like our next mode of transport is ready for us."

The helicopter's blades started up as they approached. Giles opened the back door and helped Kayli get in the back seat. He raised his thumb to the pilot, a man with a pockmarked face and short hair, and they bashed fists together to say hello. Giles ensured Kayli's safety belt was in place.

"Hi, guys. I'm Seb," the pilot said. "Are you ready back there?"

"I'm Giles, and this is my kid sister, Kayli. We're ready, mate."

"How long is the flight?" Kayli asked, her voice trembling a little.

The pilot laughed. "Hey, miss, you're in safe hands with me. We should be there within forty-five minutes, depending on the wind. Sometimes it gets up in the evening over the desert. Not the best time of year for you guys to travel to these parts. The temperature is extremely variable. It's not unheard of to be twenty-five degrees during the day and dropping down to minus eight at night."

"Minus eight? Crap, how would Mark cope with the fluctuating temperatures if he's being kept in a cave?" Kayli asked.

Giles shook his head. "I think that would be the least of his worries."

"Here we go. Hang on tight," the pilot said as the helicopter took off.

Kayli was surprised that her claustrophobia wasn't as bad in the chopper as it had been in the military plane, but she suspected that was to do with the expanse of windows in the helicopter. It didn't prevent her stomach from lurching a little though as the chopper ascended. It was a weird sensation, one that she'd never experienced in her life before. She smiled at her brother.

"You're enjoying this, aren't you?" Giles shouted in her ear.

Kayli nodded. "You know what? I think I am."

"Must be my expert flying skills," the pilot said cheekily.

They flew what seemed to be a couple of hundred feet above the ground, although Kayli suspected it was probably a lot higher than that. The pilot was skilful in his approach, weaving between the mountainous ranges as they appeared on the horizon in the failing light. As the night fully descended, Kayli's fear took hold again. She reached for Giles's hand, her sweaty palms finding it difficult to keep hold of him as her claustrophobia struck once more.

"We'll soon be there, love. Stay strong. Close your eyes. Maybe that will make you feel better."

She did as he suggested, but the bile rose into her throat instantly, and her temple broke out in sweat. Her eyes flew open again. "Is it much farther?"

"We're about ten minutes out from Kandahar. Just sit back and enjoy the ride, folks."

"I'm trying," Kayli mumbled before she glanced out the window, not that she could see anything. All of a sudden, the helicopter tilted. Panic shot up her spine. Her eyes wide, she turned to look at Giles. "What was that?"

Giles shrugged. "I haven't got a clue." He tapped the pilot on the shoulder. "Seb, everything all right?"

The pilot ignored him. The helicopter seemed to be going faster. Kayli peered out the window and into the darkness. Tiny shards of light were coming at them from the ground. She yanked on her brother's arm and pointed at the lights.

He closed his eyes and shook his head. "Shit! We're under attack. The bastards are shooting at us."

"Don't worry, folks. I've got everything under control. This happens a lot on night-time missions. I'll keep dodging the bullets as much as I can."

No sooner had Seb said that than Kayli heard a ping. Giles pulled her head into his chest to get her away from the window. Seconds later, a bullet shattered the window inches from where her head had been. Kayli screamed.

"Ssh... try to keep calm," Giles said, running a soothing hand over her head.

She tried to sit up again, but he held her down as yet more bullets struck the underside of the helicopter.

"Seb, can we escape these morons?" Giles asked.

"I'm doing my darnedest, I promise you. They're determined feckers, though. I've got this, don't worry. We're almost at the airport..."

They rounded a nearby mountain tip and Kayli saw the airport lit up ahead of them. Giles expelled a large breath and pointed ahead. She smiled, relieved to see their destination so close.

Ping, ping!

Suddenly, as if the rebels on the ground realised how close they were to landing, the firing increased.

"Keep your heads down, guys, just for the next few minutes," the pilot shouted. His head was swivelling rapidly as he glanced below him, first left and then right.

Giles's hand covered Kayli's head. She clung to her brother's waist, her ear pressed against his frantically beating heart. Closing her eyes, she tried to block out what was going on around her and focus on their mission to rescue Mark. That was proving significantly hard to do when their own lives were in jeopardy.

"Fuck! I'm hit," the pilot groaned.

Kayli tried to sit up, but Giles kept her head pinned in place. "Get off me, Giles."

Her brother removed his hand, and she sat upright.

A mixture of fear and helplessness pulled at his features. "Keep down, Kayli."

"I can't. Not when I know the pilot needs our help." She placed a hand on his shoulder and shouted, "What can we do to help you?"

"Nothing. We're going down. The chopper is losing speed and altitude. There is absolutely zilch I can do to combat that, except try to prevent her from spinning."

Kayli insisted, "Please, let us know if we can do anything. Are you hit bad?"

"No, just my arm. It's not going to help me control this girl, though."

Kayli stared at her brother. She could tell the cogs in his brain were churning rapidly as he fought to come up with a solution, but then he shook his head in dismay.

"We have to do something, Giles, or we're not going to make it."

"I know, but what? Seb needs to tell us what to do. If I could take over, I would. I've never flown a plane, let alone a chopper before."

Kayli gasped and looked out the window. The airport seemed to be so near and yet so far. "What are you saying? That we're doomed?"

"Prepare yourselves for impact, guys. I've done my best. She's about a hundred feet above the ground now and dropping fast. I'll try and keep her upright as she comes down. There's no telling if we're going to survive." Seb shouted before he cried out in pain.

Kayli wrapped her arms around her brother's neck, clinging on for dear life. It was impossible to see how close they were to the ground as the darkness of the night enveloped them.

Giles held her tightly and muttered something in her ear. It sounded as if he was praying. She hadn't prayed since she was at school. Was it right for someone to pray for their own survival? Wouldn't that seem selfish in God's eyes? She decided to pray for the pilot's and her brother's lives instead as the bullets pinged off the metal on the underside of the chopper.

The spinning started not long after.

"I'm sorry, guys. I did my best. She's hard to handle now."

"Giles, you have to help him. Grab the controls. Our lives can't end like this."

Her brother nodded. He pushed her aside and reached over the pilot's right shoulder. "Come on, Seb. Stick with it. Tell me what to do."

"Place your hands over mine. We have to keep her steady, to get out of the spin if possible."

"What about a Mayday call?" Kayli shouted.

"I was just about to do that. Giles, help me, and I'll place the call."

Kayli's mind drifted as she heard Seb's voice in the distance put in the call for help and let the authorities know where they were. Mark's face appeared before her, not the suffering Mark that had filled her dreams lately, but the happy-go-lucky, handsome Mark she'd fallen in love with all those years ago. *We're here, Mark. We're in danger, but we're trying to do everything we can.*

"Jesus. We're not going to make it!" Seb shouted, absolute fear resonating in his voice.

Kayli tried to peer through the blackness below her. "Giles, I'm scared."

Giles was too busy battling the controls with the pilot to respond. Seb groaned, and his head flopped to one side. A scream filled the helicopter... She had no idea that it had come from her own mouth until she felt the rawness in her throat. Not long after, the chopper landed with an almighty thud that sent her sprawling across the seat.

Giles began shouting at her to get out. Everything happened so fast. She was in a daze and had no idea in what order things occurred, but suddenly, she and Giles were tumbling out of the chopper. She could smell diesel all around them. With his kitbag over his shoulder, Giles grabbed her arm and yanked her away from the crash site.

She dug her heels into the sand. "No, Giles. We can't leave Seb. He needs to come with us."

"He's gone, Kayli. He's better off there. They'll just tear his body to shreds if we pull him out. Let's get out of here before she blows. The Mayday call went out. Hopefully, someone will send a search party out to find us."

"What about the rebels? We'll be sitting ducks."

"Which is why we have to take cover. Come on, sis, hold it together."

Her body trembled. She felt as though she had no control over her limbs as the shock set in. As Giles pulled her across the bumpy terrain, she stumbled now and again, but Giles's grip held firm and forced her upright. "Where are we going? We have to help Seb."

"Impossible. What we need to do is concentrate on our own survival. It's too late for Seb."

"No, I insist. We need to go back. We can't leave him there. We could bury him. There's enough sand around here."

Giles stopped and gripped her shoulders firmly. "You need to snap out of this, Kayli. Seb's dead. We need to get far away before the chopper blows."

They both looked back, and the area lit up as the fire raged through the chopper. There were no screams coming from inside.

"Okay, I'm back with you. I'm sorry, Giles. Tell me what to do." She looked sideways and noticed that he had a pistol in one of his hands.

"It's Seb's. At least it will give us some peace of mind. Look, there's a building over there. We must be on the very edge of the airport. He did his best to get us this far. The rest is up to us. Are you ready?"

"Yes. Let's do this. I'm so glad you're here with me. I couldn't do this without you, Giles."

"Nonsense. When the chips are down, you'd be able to get out of the biggest scrapes going."

"I'm not going to argue with you."

A bullet flew past the right side of her head. She let out a scream.

"Get down. We need to get to that building. Keep low and weave. Don't—whatever you do—run in a straight line. You'll be dead within seconds."

"And that's supposed to reassure me?"

"We don't have time for this. Move it."

Kayli weaved, darting left and right, some larger weaves intermingling with smaller ones. It wasn't long before they reached cover.

Giles hugged her. "You did brilliantly." He unhitched the kitbag from his shoulder, tossed it behind her then skirted forward close to the edge of the building, his gun in hand.

"Do you really think they'll send out a search party for us? Or were you just saying that to comfort me?"

He shrugged without looking at her. "Pure conjecture at this point. All we can do is sit it out here until the sun comes up and then make a move."

"Really? Wouldn't it be best to move under the cover of darkness?"

He looked over his shoulder and grinned at her. "It would be, but I didn't think you'd be up for that."

"Stop treating me like a girl and start bossing me around if you have to. I'm out of my comfort zone here, I admit, but I'm no wuss, Giles—you know that."

"I know. Duly reprimanded. Let's see if the rebels show their faces first."

She peered over his shoulder and gulped. "Shit, is that what I think it is?"

"Yep. It was only a matter of time before they took to their vehicles and came after us."

"I could do with a gun to help you fend them off."

He chuckled. "When was the last time you used a gun?"

"Hey, I'm Taser-trained. I just didn't tell you guys."

He raised an eyebrow. "That's good to know, so your aim must be fairly good then."

She slapped his back. "Cheeky sod. I might be a bit rusty, but when it comes to the crunch, I bet I could outshoot you."

"Ssh... less banter, serious heads on now," Giles whispered.

The vehicle approached at speed and stopped within thirty feet of their position. Giles placed his hand behind him, forcing Kayli back.

She scanned the immediate area, seeking something she could use as a weapon. A large plank of wood was a few feet away. She scurried towards it and dragged it back. Giles gave her the thumbs-up for using her initiative.

"Stay back. They're getting closer."

Kayli gulped as she tried to calm her erratic heartbeat. She heard the men shouting in their native tongue.

"There are only two of them," Giles whispered. "We've got this."

As the men's voices grew closer, Kayli's hand tightened around the lump of wood. She was prepared to do anything to help her brother. Once he started shooting, he would be giving their position away. That was the time she needed to prepare herself for the fight.

"Looks like they've split up," Giles whispered over his shoulder. "Last thing I want to do is start shooting at one of them."

"Use this." She placed the wood beside him. Giles edged forward a touch and swiftly pulled his head back. He lifted the wood and stood up. Kayli remained where she was but searched around her for something else she could use as a weapon. There was nothing close by except a few fist-sized rocks. She shuffled forward to retrieve a couple then swiftly returned to her position.

One of the rebels muttered something under his breath. Her own breath caught in her throat—if she could hear him, he could probably hear her. Giles stepped out in front of the man and immediately struck him several times with the piece of wood. The man's gun went off in the melee. There was no ensuing tussle between Giles and the rebel because when she looked down, she saw the wood was covered in blood, and there was a small hole in the man's forehead where a nail had struck him. She sighed then sucked in another breath as they waited for the second rebel to appear. His footsteps came closer, then he shouted at his mate.

Giles dipped his arm around the corner and shot at the rebel. The man cried out but not before he managed to fire off a couple of rounds. Giles pinned himself against the building. When he thought it was safe, he poked his head around the corner and gave Kayli the all-clear signal.

She followed him over to the bodies, shame and compassion her prominent emotions. Giles kicked the men's bodies, looking for some kind of reaction, but there was none.

"Kayli, get my bag. Can you manage to carry it?"

"Of course I can." She picked up the bag, slipped her arms through the straps, and hoisted it onto her back while Giles relieved the men of their weapons and ammunition. "What now?"

Giles patted the men's pockets and extracted a wallet from one of them. "Sorry, mate. Our need is greater than yours."

"I never thought we'd have to resort to robbing the dead," Kayli said, shaking her head in disbelief.

"Get over it, and quickly. Needs must in these parts, sis. Come on. I was actually looking for the keys to the vehicle. They must have left them in the ignition, but the cash will come in handy for buying food."

"You obviously have it all planned out. I'm out of my depth around here."

He ran towards the vehicle. "We need to get out of here."

Kayli, in spite of the heavy load on her back, ran after him.

Once they were at the jeep, Giles removed the kitbag and threw it in the back of the vehicle. "Climb in. I have no idea how far this heap is going to carry us, but we need to get out of here before someone comes searching for those men."

"Aren't we supposed to be meeting someone?"

"Yep, let's get to the airport. I'll contact our guys from there."

She placed her hand on his arm as he started the jeep. "Thank you for saving us."

He leaned over and kissed her on the cheek. "It's what big brothers do, isn't it?"

"Not always. I appreciate it, though."

CHAPTER TWELVE

The journey was one of the bumpiest Kayli had ever endured. The jeep was a wreck. The seats were ripped, and their lack of padding made her regret her recent weight loss. Maybe Dave was right about her bum being too bony, after all.

Giles chuckled. "Not the smoothest of rides, granted. However, if it gets us from A to B, it'll do for me."

"I'm not complaining, I promise. Anything is better than setting off on foot. We're nearly there, right?"

"Yep, not far. We still need to be careful—there could be rebels all around the airport for all we know."

"Do you want to dump the vehicle soon? Where were we supposed to meet up with your contact?"

"At the airport. I'll give them a ring once we've stopped."

Giles drove another five hundred yards and drew up behind a huge hangar. He withdrew his mobile and tapped in a number. "Hey, Jacko. We're here. Change of plan, though. The pilot crashed and was killed. We've got rebels on our tails... Okay, we're hiding out behind one of the large hangars at the end of the airport. That's as good as it gets, mate. Can't give you a more definite location than that... Right, see you soon." Giles disconnected the call. "It's a waiting game now. Just remain vigilant."

Kayli covered her face with her hands. "Oh gosh, do you think we've done the right thing coming out here?"

Giles withdrew her hands from her face and held them firmly in his own. "Don't go doubting the mission, not yet. We've had a minor blip. That's all."

"Three dead bodies in the last twenty minutes, and you call that a *minor* blip?"

Giles glared at her and held her gaze. "You need to toughen up, and quickly, love. No self-doubts from here on out. Got that? Remember what we're hoping to achieve at the end of this mission?

We both recognised the dangers before we left the UK, right? Just remember why we're risking our lives. Mark needs us. Keep that at the forefront of your mind at all times."

Kayli nodded and extracted her hands from his. "Sorry for my mini-meltdown. I promise not to do it again. I realise I've got to toughen up. It's hard to get past the guilt I feel for leaving the pilot back there."

He shook his head. "It was better for him to go up in flames. If the men had dragged him out of the chopper, they would have beheaded him and chopped his body to pieces. They're savages in this part of the world. Half the stories you hear back home in the media are tampered down for the sake of the victims' families. Trust me, you need to keep on your toes at all times out here. You're going to have to perfect sleeping with one eye open. I'll do my best to keep you within reach but there are going to be times when that just won't be possible, like when you need to go to the toilet. It's imperative that you're aware of what's going on around you every second of every minute. Am I making myself clear?"

"All right. There's no need to speak to me like that, Giles. I'm not stupid. Sorry for showing emotions because a man lost his life because of us today. It won't happen again."

He pulled her into his arms. "No, it's me who should be sorry. I just needed you to be aware of the truth. If these guys capture you, then..."

"I understand. I'll do everything I can to ensure that doesn't happen."

"Ditto." He lifted a handful of her hair. "You're going to hate me for saying this. I should have brought it up sooner, but maybe you should consider getting rid of your hair."

She gasped and snatched the clump of hair from his hand. "I can't do that. It's taken me years to grow it this long." *Does he realise what he's asking?*

"It gives the game away that you're female. If you cut it off, then you could get away with being a male, less of a target for them to pick out when the chips are down. It's your choice, of course."

A girl parting with her hair at the drop of a hat! Why the hell didn't he suggest it when we were at home, when I had a pair of scissors to hand? She knew she should listen to him and how ludicrous it was not to consider what he was saying, but her head was all over the place. Nothing about this situation was making her think straight. *Mark would kill me. He loves my hair being long.* "I'll think about it," she replied sullenly.

Giles decided they would be better off away from the vehicle, hiding between the buildings, until his contacts arrived.

Standing in the same position for the next thirty minutes caused Kayli's legs to burn, but every time she moved Giles ordered her to stay still. When she heard another vehicle approaching, she froze and stared at her brother. Giles placed a finger to his lips. Kayli nodded.

Giles withdrew his vibrating phone from his pocket. "Jacko, is that you? Okay, we're coming out." He hung up. "It's fine. It's our boys. We'll be safe now, for the time being anyway." He picked up the kitbag sitting on the ground beside Kayli.

She pulled at it and said, "You keep the weapons handy. I'll carry the bag as agreed."

They emerged from behind the building and walked towards the vehicle. A heavyset man was standing alongside the four-door car that, at a quick glance, looked like a Mercedes. His gaze shifted between Kayli and Giles, mostly falling on her. Despite the chill in the evening air, warmth crept into her cheeks.

Giles shook the man's hand then pulled him into a manly hug before he introduced her. "I'd like you to meet my skinny blister, Kayli."

Jacko's eyes narrowed. "I've heard a lot about you DI Bright of the Avon and Somerset Constabulary. One thing before we set off. You're out of your jurisdiction here and there's only one person in charge around here. That's me. As long as you adhere to that, we should get along fine."

"I appreciate that, Jacko. You'll have no problems from me. However, if I think of a better solution to a scenario along the way, I will be voicing my opinion. Of course, it'll be down to you whether you take my advice or not."

Giles pulled one side of his jacket over his face to disguise his grin and Jacko's eyes narrowed even more. He took two steps towards Kayli and lowered his face to hers. She gulped.

He thrust out his hand for her to shake and laughed. "I love ballsy women. You and I are going to get along just fine. Feel free to chip in when you like. I'm not promising we'll take your advice, but we'll still value your opinion, that is until the bullets start flying—then you keep your mouth shut and follow orders."

"Sounds like a plan to me. Good to meet you, and thank you for agreeing to help us find Mark."

"We never leave a man behind, whether he's still with the army or if he's moved on to pastures new."

Kayli smiled. She liked this man. "That's good to know."

"Hey, guys. It's nice that you're getting acquainted. But, do you mind if we do that elsewhere?" a gruff voice called out from inside the vehicle.

"The troops are getting restless. I'll stick your bag in the boot. Hop in, the pair of you, and introduce yourselves to the uglier members of the team."

"We heard that, dipshit. I've had more girlfriends than you've had shaves, Jacko."

"Yeah, you might have done, Bandy. Pray tell us, how many of those poor unfortunate women stuck around for a second shag?"

Kayli burst into laughter when she heard the man inside the vehicle curse at Jacko.

Giles whispered in her ear. "If Jacko likes you, then you're doing well. Get in." He held the back door open for her, and Kayli slid in beside a man with a closely shaven head. He had muscles on his muscles, and one of his thighs was the size of her waist.

He turned to look at her, and his gaze dropped to take in the length of her body before he held out his hand. "So you're Giles's kid sister. I'm Mac. Pleased to meet you."

"Hi, Mac. Thanks for helping us."

"Don't thank me until we get Mark back, then you can buy us all a steak dinner."

Kayli chuckled. "You've got yourself a deal."

Giles squeezed in beside her. "Shift over a bit. My bum is bigger than yours, sis."

Kayli moved along the seat so that her leg was touching Mac's. She mumbled an apology.

"Hey, don't apologise. I love it when a good-looking female sidles up to me."

Giles laughed. "Leave her alone, Mac. She'd wipe the floor with you, mate."

They all laughed. The other man sitting in the front seat swivelled to look at her. "I guess I'll have to introduce myself. I'm Bandy. Don't ask. Good to meet you. Keep your head down when we tell you to, and we should all get along just fine."

"Nice to meet you, Bandy."

Jacko eased himself behind the steering wheel and drove off. The men's banter on their journey had Kayli in fits at times. If this was what the camaraderie was like on patrol in the army, she understood now why Mark had found it impossible to adjust to civilian life. She promised to be more understanding once he was safe and back home with her in the UK. Giles nudged her leg and winked at her. She smiled back, reassuring him that the men had made her feel welcome and that she was pretty relaxed about being there with them.

"Can I ask what you guys are doing out here?" Kayli asked.

"We're in a covert operation to find a group of ISIS scumbags. The main group is on their tails. Giles put in a call a few weeks back to say that our old mate Mark had been captured, and our commanding officer appointed us as your babysitters. That's it."

"Babysitters, my arse." Giles laughed and jabbed Mac in his thigh with his fist.

"It is what it is, mate. Are you regretting going back to civvie street yet?"

"Nope. I've got another kid on the way. Life's all good at my end."

"Awesome news. Fuck, I bet your missus had a right go at your nuts when you told her you were coming back out here."

Giles sighed. "Yeah, things were a little strained, but she knows how important it was for us to come. She'll be right when we return home unharmed and with Mark in tow."

Kayli squeezed her brother's hand.

"So you're a cop. How long have you been doing that, Kayli?" Mac asked, obviously the most inquisitive of the group.

"About eight years now. Kind of lose track of time after a while."

"Take you long to become an inspector, did it?"

"Around five years, which isn't bad for a woman."

"You must have something about you then, unless you have an appreciative male superior who enjoys having your pretty face around the place."

Giles sucked in air beside her. "Ouch, sexist comments like that could get you into big trouble, Mac."

Kayli shrugged. "I'm used to it, Giles. I used to get a lot of flack from my fellow male officers until my team started coming top every year for meeting their targets. Hey, Mac, for your information, my superior officer is a woman. Don't think she gives me an easy ride, either. If anything, she comes down harder on me than my fellow male inspectors."

"How come?"

"She knows how difficult it is being a female officer in the force. It takes balls and determination to put up with all the sexist remarks confronting us from male colleagues who doubt our abilities."

The men all laughed. "Consider yourself told, Mac," Jacko shouted. "Now stop winding her up and leave her alone. We're almost there, guys. It's a bit of a dive, so don't expect too much."

"Don't worry about it. As long as we're able to get our heads down for a couple of hours, that's fine by us. Right, sis?"

"Of course. Not sure I'll be able to sleep, though," Kayli replied.

"You will," Giles assured her.

The car drew up outside a white house that formed part of a terrace. They left the car and entered the gate that opened up onto a drab courtyard. Kayli cringed at the sight of bullet holes in the house's façade. *Does this mean they are sitting targets?* She tried not to dwell on that too much and followed Mac and Giles into the house, while Jacko and Bandy brought up the rear. Giles dropped his kitbag on the floor in the first room they entered—actually, it was the only room on the ground floor. The tiled floor with its garish pattern did very little to create a warm and friendly interior. There were no pictures on the walls or curtains at the windows. Every wall was painted white but showed signs of the gun battles that had taken place over the months or years. Piles of dust filled the corners where someone had swept the room but had neglected to clear it up. Kayli resisted the urge to search for a dustpan and brush. She couldn't be regarded as a domestic goddess by any stretch of the imagination, but the temptation to rid the place of dust set her teeth on edge for some unknown reason.

"This is it, I'm afraid. There's another level, but you'll be risking life and limb to get to it," Jacko announced. "Sorry it's not the Ritz, Kayli."

She smiled and waved a hand in front of her. "As long as there's running water to have a quick wash, that's all I need."

Jacko shook his head. "Maybe you didn't notice the stench of BO in the car. There's no such thing, not here anyway. There's a public toilet down the road, and we tend to go there when the smell gets too bad."

"Good job I brought a can of deodorant with me and a good supply of fresh knickers."

Giles jabbed her in the ribs. "Too much information, sis. We'll get you to the toilets in one piece when the need arises."

"I can go by myself, Giles. I'm not an invalid."

Her brother raised his eyebrow. "I never said you were. It's far too dangerous out there for you to be walking the streets."

"Okay, I think I realised that much all by myself. Any chance of a coffee?"

Giles rolled his eyes. "Don't you ever think of anything else?"

"What can I say? I'm addicted."

Bandy moved to the far side of the room and held up a canister. "Coffee. We've got a small camping gas stove here. Mac, can you get the water topped up for us?"

Mac picked up the jerrycan in the corner and left the house. He returned five minutes later and handed the can to Bandy, who promptly poured the water into a battered metal kettle and lit the gas stove with a match.

Kayli started to laugh, making everyone pause to look in her direction. "Sorry, guys. I've just got this image of a warped edition of *Carry On Camping*."

The men roared with laughter. Giles winked at her, letting her know that response meant she'd been accepted by the group.

Over coffee and a few stale sandwiches one of the guys had found in one of the kitbags, Kayli listened intently to the men. They described in gruesome detail the battles they and their comrades had encountered while in Afghanistan. The heinous crimes ISIS had subjected the locals to. They also briefly filled her in on the recent history of the conflict in the area, including how the coalition forces had rid most of the nearby areas of ISIS during an operation that took place in 2016. How the Taliban had become prevalent once more, intent on recapturing their country. The upshot of that meant the locals still feared what was going to happen to their country and had no idea whether the insurgents still walked amongst them. According to Mac, coalition soldiers had discovered a special radio station broadcasting farewell messages from children as young as eight before they set off on suicide missions, driving cars into the heart of hugely populated areas. The kids had been brainwashed into thinking they would be far better off in the afterlife. Kayli wiped away a tear when she heard this.

Kayli frowned. "Can I ask an obvious question?" The men nodded. "How are you guys supposed to know who the allies are and who the enemy is, when they live amongst the people in communities such as this?"

"That's the trouble—we don't," Jacko said. "Some bloke could one day provide us with information about a secret Taliban or ISIS hideout and lead us to that location, the next day, he could be carrying a gun and shooting at us. There's no rhyme or reason for us to be here. If these guys want to live like this and tear each other apart, then in my opinion, we should get out of the country and leave them to get on with it. We've done our part by training the coalition soldiers. Ha, 'soldiers' might be stretching the imagination a little."

"What do you mean?" Kayli tilted her head. She needed to understand the psyche of the people surrounding them, because she sensed any information she gathered would come in useful once Mark was within their sights.

"We had the misfortune of working alongside some of these guys a few weeks back. They point a machine gun and aim at a building." He indicated the holes in the wall all around them. "Until they've emptied all their ammunition. Then they sit back, laughing. Don't get me wrong, you'll get the odd ones amongst them who go about their roles seriously, but nine times out of ten, they treat war as a joke. A life means fuck-all in these parts."

"That's so sad. Do you think they'll ever be free of militant forces?" Kayli asked.

Mac snorted. "They might get rid of one lot, but within days, an even worse group will emerge. Everyone thought the Taliban were the cruellest bastards to walk this earth, but then ISIS formed and put paid to that notion. They really are the scum of this world. Whatever the Taliban did, ISIS can top it and multiply it by a thousand."

Giles cringed beside her. She reached over and squeezed his hand. "I know what you're thinking. I had to hear what we're going to be up against, Giles."

"I know, sis. Hey, just remember you've got a crack team around you. The second we hear where Mark is being held, we'll swoop."

"I just wanted to tell you all how much this means to me. I promise not to hinder your operation, if there is one. Speaking for Mark and myself, I can't thank you enough for risking your lives like this to rescue him."

"Save your thanks until we find him," Jacko said with a smile. "Right, sup up, guys. We need to get some shuteye. We'll take it in turn to stand guard. I'll take the first slot."

The men organised how they were going to guard the building, swapping over the watch after a two-hour stint. Kayli wanted to volunteer her services but knew they would think she was out of her mind, so she remained silent.

She and Giles huddled up together. Surprisingly, sleep descended almost immediately. She stirred when Mac shook Giles awake, telling him to stand guard at the window overlooking the yard. Giles, ever the protective big brother, kissed her forehead and placed his kitbag under her head. She soon drifted off to sleep again.

Her brother woke her up with a steaming cup of coffee early the next morning. "Hello, princess. Did you sleep well?"

Kayli stretched the knots out of her back and yawned. "I suppose I was more tired than I first thought. Are you all right?"

"I'm fine. No need to worry about me." She looked over at Jacko, who entered the front door, carrying a couple of paper bags.

He deposited the bags in the middle of the room.

"Dig in, guys. It's only fresh fruit, all I could muster at this time of the morning."

Kayli chose a huge bright-green apple and bit into it. "Thanks, I really appreciate it."

"Don't mention it," Jacko replied.

Giles dipped into his back pocket and pulled out the wallet he'd stolen from the soldier he'd killed. "Here, you might as well add this to the pot. I haven't got a clue how much is in there. We acquired it last night. I figured it was useless to the guy I shot."

"All contributions gratefully received." Jacko laughed and put the wallet in the back pocket of his combat trousers.

Giles nodded. "What's the plan for today?"

"We've got the feelers out with the locals. Information comes to us in dribs and drabs, and it's up to us to figure out if the information is real or not. Some of these guys take pleasure in toying with us." Jacko's phone rang. He answered it as he rushed out of the house and into the courtyard.

Kayli ran over to the window to watch him. She saw his face turn red with anger as he flung his free arm up in the air. *Shit! What if someone is telling him that Mark is dead? I don't think I'll be able to face that. My need to find him has become even greater since my arrival in this godforsaken country.* She returned to stand alongside her brother when she saw Jacko end his call. Moments later, he entered the house. His gaze focussed on a cracked tile in the floor a few feet in front of him.

"Come on, man, hit us with it," Mac demanded.

Jacko sighed. "Guys, we better make the next forty-eight hours count. I've just been told they're shipping us back to the UK."

CHAPTER THIRTEEN

Kayli gripped Giles's arm, frantic at the implications behind Jacko's announcement.

Giles slipped an arm around her shoulder and pulled her close. "Don't worry. We can do this, sis. Soldiers thrive on being put under pressure, just like you do. We've got this covered, I promise you."

She shook her head in disbelief. "How can you say that? We have no idea where Mark is even being held. Are we likely to stumble across that kind of information? Please enlighten me how that's going to happen, because I'm at a bloody loss to know right now, brother dearest."

"Calm down and stop making a scene." Giles looked over his shoulder at the others. "Everyone in this room is going to go the extra mile to find Mark before they're shipped back to the UK. You have my word on that."

"Mine too," Jacko added. "We're issued with orders like this all the time. If we can locate where Mark is being held in the meantime, that deadline could be shifted—delayed a few days at least—until we've rescued him. You have my word we won't let you down. Mark's one of us. If he's out there, we'll find him."

Kayli smiled at Jacko. "I'm sorry. I went into panic mode then. I know this is going to sound daft, but recently, I've been having dreams about Mark, where he speaks to me, tells me that they're starving him to death. If those dreams hadn't happened, I wouldn't be here now. I'm willing to do anything, to risk my life, in order to help save his."

Jacko took a few steps towards her. "That's admirable of you. The best thing you can do, Kayli, is keep the faith. We've never failed a mission yet, and we're not about to start now."

"Thank you."

Giles hooked his arm through hers. "Excuse us for a moment, gents." He guided her outside into the courtyard and gathered her in his arms. Struggling to keep hold of her emotions, she buried her head in his chest. Giles had always been able to read her innermost feelings during their childhood. "Let it out, love. I have faith in the boys. They won't let us down."

She pulled away, and their gazes met. "I hope not. Now I'm here, I have a very bad feeling about this, Giles. I hope I'm wrong. Do you think their contacts will come through?"

"If Jacko says they can rely on a few of the locals, then we have to believe him. These guys are aware of the dangers out here. The best thing we can do is trust their judgement. You have my word that they'll bust their bollocks to do the right thing for Mark."

"Thanks, I needed to hear that. Where do we go from here?" she asked.

"It's a waiting game until one of their contacts gets in touch. That could be today or tomorrow. There's just no telling. I know that won't make you feel any better, knowing that we're up against the clock now, but you need to have confidence in Jacko and the boys. They're the experts in this theatre."

"I do have faith in them. They seem a good bunch. I hope I haven't upset the applecart by being too girly around them."

"You haven't. Just try and hold it together. You're doing well so far."

"Thanks. I want him back, Giles. He's desperate for our help."

"He's getting our help. Come on, let's rejoin the others."

They walked back into the house. The three occupants were all busy on their phones, and Kayli felt relieved they were able to slink into the room without drawing their attention.

The afternoon dragged by. They all took their turn pacing around the room, waiting for someone to reach out to share some information. Kayli took it upon herself to keep the men supplied with coffee.

Mac's phone rang as dusk arrived. All eyes fell on him, as everyone was eager to hear any news. He turned his back on the group to finish his conversation.

After the call had ended, he punched the air. "One of my contacts thinks he knows where Mark is. I've asked him to join us here. He's on his way."

Kayli's heart squeezed with joy. She glanced at her brother, unsure how to react.

Giles nodded and smiled. "This is the moment we've been waiting for, sis."

She exhaled a large breath and sank to the floor, not sure if her legs would be able to hold her upright for much longer.

They waited impatiently for the man to arrive. At ten minutes to eight, the catch on the gate in the courtyard squeaked. The men all reached for their weapons, and Giles took up his position in front of Kayli, shielding her.

Mac marched towards the door, his weapon resting against his cheek. He opened the door and beckoned the man inside. Sweat glistening on his brow, the man was dressed in grubby white trousers and a baggy shirt. His gaze darted around the room.

"Stand down, men," Jacko ordered.

The soldiers lowered their weapons to their sides but still kept them to hand as the man tentatively entered the room. Kayli's detective skills put his demeanour down to guilt. But that would have been back in the UK. She didn't have a clue how the locals acted in situations like this, especially when confronted by armed soldiers. *Maybe he's sweating because he's run all the way here. Perhaps I'm doing him an injustice.*

He smiled hesitantly at everyone in the room. "Guys, this is Abdul." Mac slapped the man on the back as he made the introductions. "Do you want a coffee?"

The man shook his head erratically. "No. I need get back. My family needs me."

"I understand. What can you tell us, Abdul?" Mac asked.

The man's gaze lingered on Kayli. His eyes narrowed for a few seconds before his gaze continued to drift around the room, taking in the soldiers and their weapons. Kayli had to dig deep to resist the urge to shudder. Despite Giles's warning that women were treated differently in these parts, she hadn't expected to feel like that under a local's stare. She knew what she had to do once they were alone again. But that would have to wait. She bit down on her tongue as she waited for Mac and the others to start questioning the man. He was very fidgety, shifting his weight from one leg to the other. Once he'd glanced around the room, his eyes settled on Kayli again. This time, she felt his stare go deeper, as though he were reaching into her soul. She shuddered, unable to prevent the unpleasant feeling rising within her.

Sensing her anguish, Giles took a step closer to Kayli. His arm touched hers without it being too obvious. The man's glare ceased, and he spoke to Mac. "I know where UK soldier is being kept. I need to check before I give you information. My family haven't eaten a good meal in days."

Jacko withdrew his wallet and handed the man a few notes. Abdul's eyes bulged, and he tucked the money swiftly in his trouser pocket. "Where?" Jacko demanded.

"In house in Kandahar. I have man outside, spying for me. He need money also."

Jacko tutted, dipped into his wallet again, and gave the man a few more notes.

Abdul nodded. "I make contact when I can. I need to go. Need feed my hungry wife and children."

Mac walked out of the house with him.

Kayli eyed Giles, unsure whether she should share what was eating at her or not.

Giles cocked an eyebrow. "Come on, let's hear what's on your mind, sis?"

She inhaled a large breath and let it out slowly before she replied, "I know this isn't what you guys want to hear, but if that fella walked into my police station, I'd be very wary of anything he told me."

Giles laughed. "Ever the suspicious detective."

She slapped his arm. "I'm being deadly serious about this, Giles."

"Noted. You don't think he was acting suspiciously because of our weapons?" Jacko asked.

She shook her head then shrugged. "Maybe it's me being overly suspicious. All I know is that his mannerisms would lead me to distrust anything he says."

"So, you're telling us that he hasn't got a wife and kids at home who haven't had a square meal in days?" Jacko's mouth twitched with what looked like amusement.

"Did he look starved to you? Yes, he might seem a little on the thin side, but I'd hardly place him in the starving category."

Jacko tapped his foot. "Hmm... maybe your sister has got a point, Giles."

"How well do you know him, Mac?" Giles asked.

Mac hitched up his right shoulder. "Not very well. Must admit that's the first time he's mentioned a wife and kids to me, as far as I can remember anyway."

"In that case, maybe we should be wary about what he tells us," Jacko said.

Kayli's head sank onto her chest then rose again. Her hands flew out to the side and slapped against her thighs. She felt confused. "But what if I'm wrong about this? Haven't you guys got any feelings about this guy?"

Mac shook his head. "I've known him a few months. Every piece of intel he's ever given me has been accurate. I say we believe him, but act on what he tells us with caution."

"I think Mac is right. It's not as if we've got other options open to us at this point," Bandy agreed.

"I'm with the boys," Jacko said.

Kayli shrugged. "However you want to proceed is fine by me. Perhaps I should have kept my mouth shut in the first place."

Giles nudged her arm with his. "I'm sure the guys wouldn't want you to do that. I vote that we listen to what Abdul has to say when he gets in touch, and do our best to verify what he says first before we act upon it."

"Agreed. Not sure how we're going to manage that, but I think you're right, mate," Jacko said.

Kayli scanned the area and spotted a knife in Bandy's belt. She crossed the floor and smiled at the man before she removed the knife. He stepped back and raised his hands.

"Crap, don't kill me for agreeing with my comrades," he joked.

Kayli poked her tongue out at him and held the knife out in front of her. "Who's going to do the honours?"

The men eyed each other in puzzlement, wondering if she'd lost her mind.

"Come on, guys, unless anyone has got a pair of scissors, that is."

The men only looked more confused.

"We haven't got a Scooby-Doo what you're going on about, love," Jacko said.

She sighed heavily. "Giles and I discussed this last night. I saw the way that man looked at me, and he's supposed to be our ally. God knows how the Taliban or ISIS bastards are going to react when they lay eyes on me. One of you needs to hack off my hair. Who's going to volunteer to do it?"

"Hey, I think you're right. Maybe one of us should do it rather than Giles," Bandy replied.

"That's what I was thinking, because if Giles did it, he'd feel my wrath for the rest of his days," Kayli joked.

Bandy stepped forward and removed the knife from her hand. "I've always fancied myself as a barber. Hey, maybe we should get the razor out and give you a blade-one haircut instead of using the knife. What do you say, Kayli?"

"Crap, I'm regretting my decision already," she replied nervously.

Giles laughed. "A quick slice will be all it takes, sis. However, it's going to take you years to regrow it."

"Don't I know it, and with a wedding to look forward to next year too." She winked at him, trying to keep her spirits upbeat. She stood with her back to Bandy, her eyes closed tightly as if she were about to undergo the most terrifying torture treatment ever discovered by man.

Bandy pressed her head forward then grabbed her hair and pulled on it. She felt the knife slice through her luscious locks. Moments later, Bandy presented her with the offcut. Tears filled her eyes. There was no going back.

She glanced over at her brother, who was standing with his mouth hanging open. "Do you think Mark will still recognise me when he sees me?" *Do you think he'll still love me and want to marry me?* she was desperate to add.

The men all laughed, and Giles crossed the room to hug her. "No doubt about it, love. He'll regard you as his heroine whether you have your beautiful long hair or not. You're still the most caring, loving person you were before. He'll realise that from the get-go."

Kayli smiled and wiped away the few tears that had dripped onto her cheek. "I can't believe I just did that. I suppose we all have to make sacrifices in this life. I think that was a major one for me. How do I look?"

"As beautiful as ever. I bet Mum and Dad will have trouble recognising you when we get back."

"Shit! Do I look that different? Is it too masculine?"

"Hey, that was your intention, right?" Mac called over.

She grimaced. "Ouch! I suppose so. Okay, what's done is done. Now what?" She tried to shrug off one of the hardest decisions she'd ever had to make in her life. *I'm overreacting. It's just a bunch of hair. It'll regrow. It's not as if I've just cut off my arm or my leg, for God's sake. Get a grip, girl.*

"We sit and wait for Abdul to get back to us. I think you're right. We'll treat the information he gives us with caution. I've never had a reason to distrust him in the past, but that doesn't mean to say we shouldn't consider it going forward. The rebels might have got to him. When a Westerner's life is at risk, it kind of puts a different spin on things all round."

Kayli took the band from her hair and let it fall loose. Instead of her mane falling down to her waist, it was now barely touching her shoulders. She couldn't remember the last time she had worn it so short, possibly in her teens at school. She held up the offcut and said to Giles, "All right if I put it in the bag and take it home as a souvenir of our trip?" She was determined to keep her mood buoyant to cover the fact that inside, she felt as though she'd lost a limb. She knew how ridiculous that sounded in the grand scheme of things when people around her were losing their lives, but she struggled to get past her emotions, which were all over the place in her new surroundings.

Mac handed her a hip flask. "Here, you look as though you could do with a proper drink."

Kayli took a swig of the burning liquid, lowered the flask, and had a coughing fit, much to the men's amusement. "Crap! What kind of shit is that?"

"Their own brand of whisky. It's not very refined, is it?"

She handed the flask back to Mac. "Thanks, I think."

Her act of self-sacrifice helped her bond with the group of men. Over the course of the evening, they asked her about her role as a DI and how she came to join the force instead of choosing the army like her brother.

"To be honest, I've never thought about joining the army. Maybe that has something to do with being brought up by a general and moving from country to country every couple of years. Perhaps Giles appreciated that side of his childhood more than I did. I can't really tell you the reason behind me joining the force." She fell silent as she thought back. No one had ever really asked her that question. "Wait... there was quite a high-profile case in the news about a serial killer bumping off prostitutes in the Suffolk area that caught my interest when I was in my teens. I suppose that must have sparked more than my imagination at the time."

"How do you get on with your male counterparts?" Bandy asked. "The reason I raise the question is because a distant relative of mine joined the force about twenty years ago. She found it really tough. Actually, she left after a couple of years, found it impossible to work alongside the blokes. She said they were treated differently to her, if I recall."

"I can understand her saying that. Back then, I think it was super tough being a female copper. Maybe it's better now because some of those women serving during your relative's time on the force went on to become DCIs and DIs. My own DCI is a prime example. Sometimes she's really tough on me, but I know she's only doing it for my own good."

"Kayli's a top-notch inspector, guys. She runs a tight ship and has an excellent arrest record. She's just too modest to share that piece of news."

Kayli smiled at him. "I love that you've always got my back, bro."

"Too right, and I know that's reciprocated."

Kayli smiled. "It is. Anyway, I'm hoping to have a job to go back to upon my return."

"Is there any doubt about that?" Mac asked. "What with you being so proficient?"

"I'm not sure. I suppose there's always that niggling doubt in my mind. My DCI willingly suggested I take two weeks' holiday. Some holiday, right, guys?" She sniggered.

The men laughed. "You know what, Kayli? You're an all right kind of girl. Mark should count himself lucky for having you in his corner. Not every girl would go above and beyond the way you have. Risking their lives to rescue their fella," Jacko said, a look of admiration in his dark-brown eyes.

Kayli's cheeks flushed. "Thanks, guys. That means a lot coming from you."

"Time for some scran. Bandy and I will go. Mac, you stay here with these guys. Everyone hungry?" Jacko asked.

The room filled with raised thumbs and enthusiastic nods. Kayli watched the two men leave, but her stomach tied in knots pretty soon after, as she was fearful when the group parted. She needn't have worried, though, as Giles and Mac armed themselves and stood guard at the window and the door until Bandy and Jacko returned.

In their absence, Kayli had gathered the few plates they had and given them a quick wash.

Jacko and Bandy entered the house again twenty minutes later. The smell of roasted meat wafted into the room with them. Kayli's stomach growled. She was hungrier than she'd realised. Jacko handed her two bags. One contained a round loaf of bread, and the other a chicken that had been roasted and was coated in all sorts of spices.

She divided the meal, taking a smaller portion for herself, and handed the plates around. Ravenous, they all tucked into the feast. At first, she was unsure whether she liked the spices, but with each mouthful, the taste grew on her. The bread was harder than she was expecting, and sometimes, if she took a large bite, it got lodged in her throat.

They were nearing the end of the meal when Mac's phone rang. He hurriedly answered it and placed the call on speaker. "Abdul, what do you have for us?"

Everyone's attention was drawn to what the man was telling them.

"I hear he's going to be moved tonight."

"Where are they moving him from?" Mac asked.

"Close to library in town. They keep him in house in alley there."

"Do you know where they're taking him?"

"I hear Kabul."

Mac's brow furrowed. "Why Kabul?"

"I know not why. The Taliban know you in area."

"When?" Mac asked the only other question that needed to be asked.

"In twenty minutes. You must hurry. I go now." With that, their contact hung up.

Kayli's gaze darted between the men. "Do we believe him?"

Giles shrugged. "We have to. It's all we have."

Jacko nodded. "Agreed. We need to ensure we're properly armed, plenty of backup ammo before we set off. Move it."

Kayli stood up and watched the men load their weapons, unsure what her role should be.

Giles stood alongside her and smiled. "This is it, sis. Hopefully, we'll get Mark back without much hassle."

"What do you need me to do? Can I have a weapon? I'm coming with you, right? I don't want to be left behind."

Jacko tapped his gun once it was loaded. "You'll come with us, but stay in the car in case there's a shoot-out."

"Okay," was all she could think of to say as her mind whirled and her heart rate escalated at the thought of seeing her fella within a matter of minutes.

Giles's arm crushed her to him. "We've got this, Kayli. We'll be on the plane back to Blighty soon. I promise you."

CHAPTER FOURTEEN

They left the house and piled into the car, Jacko and Bandy up front and Mac and Giles either side of her in the rear. Moments later, they parked in the road next to the library. They had a good view of the alley Abdul had mentioned, but darkness had descended, making it impossible to see.

Jacko hit the steering wheel. "We're going to have to get closer. Can't take the risk of them leaving here. Agreed?"

Please, don't put Mark's life in danger. The words rattled around her head, but she knew better than to voice them. The men would do everything they could not to endanger Mark's life further.

Giles leaned over to whisper, "You should come with us. Stick behind me—close, all right?"

Kayli's head bobbed up and down, her eyes wide with a mixture of fear and excitement at the thought of seeing Mark after all these weeks.

"Are you ready, guys? On the count of three. One... two... three." Jacko rallied his men into attack mode.

The five of them flew out the car. Kayli grabbed her brother's jacket and stuck to him like glue. They found a safe position close to the library and watched the other men sneak closer in the darkness. A car's lights lit up ahead, and the men darted for cover.

"We can't let them get away, Giles," Kayli whispered.

"They won't. Let us deal with this, sis."

"Okay. I'll keep quiet."

They heard men laughing, close to the vehicle ahead. The car door opened, adding extra light to the alley. Kayli's heart was in her mouth when two men removed a hooded man from the building and shoved him into the back of the car. "My God, it's him. Why aren't Jacko and his men attacking them? Please, please don't let them get away."

"Ssh... keep quiet. Let us think."

Kayli saw Jacko and Bandy crouch and begin to move down the alley towards the car. Mac remained where he was on the other side of the alley, his machine gun placed across his arm, aimed at the vehicle.

"I hope they're going to make a move soon," Kayli whispered in her brother's ear as she peered over his shoulder.

"Be patient and ssh..."

The men got into the car, then the engine started up. Kayli gripped Giles's shoulder. He shrugged her off and kept his position intact, aiming at the car's tyres.

Seconds later, Jacko and Bandy ran at the vehicle, shouting at the men to get out of the car. Gunshots were fired. Everything was a daze for Kayli once she heard the guns going off, and unexpected tears dripped onto her cheeks. *Please be careful. Don't hurt Mark!*

Mac ran down the alley to join the others as yet more gunshots were fired. "Giles, we need to get in there. What if the Taliban kill Mark rather than let him escape?"

"Ssh... it's all in hand. Be patient."

After more gunshots, Kayli heard men shouting Allah's name. She couldn't stand it any longer. She broke cover and ran down the alley.

"Come back here, Kayli, you idiot."

More shots were fired, then there was silence. In the silence, Kayli heard only her heavy breathing and the sound of running feet. Bandy pulled her arm before she reached the vehicle.

"Don't go any closer, Kayli. Stand down."

"I'm not one of your men. I have a right to be here. I need to see if Mark is okay."

Jacko stood in front of her, his eyes blazing into hers. "Stand back. That's an order."

Kayli covered her mouth with her hand as Jacko and Bandy cautiously approached the car. They opened the back door, and Bandy shot into the car. Kayli's heart skipped several beats and her breath caught in her throat.

Giles arrived and yanked her round to face him. "Don't you ever do that to me again, you hear me?"

She nodded. Her gaze shot back to the car as Jacko reached into the back seat. Giles rushed past Kayli. They hauled the hooded man out of the vehicle, and Giles removed the cloth from his head. Kayli's legs gave way beneath her. She rocked back and forth as tears cascaded down her cheeks. It wasn't him. Mark was gone. They had been led into a trap.

The man was grinning at them. Giles punched him in the mouth. His head snapped back then quickly returned to the same position. He glared at Giles, blood dripping from his mouth, and spat at him. Then he started shouting in his own language. Every other word was Allah, or so it seemed to Kayli.

Mac helped her to her feet. "Come on, don't let him see how much you're affected by his vile actions. Show strength even in your weakest moment. Don't let the bastards think they've won."

"But they have won. For all we know, Mark is dead. Why do that? Why toy with us like this?"

"They're a different brand of soldier. They're cowards, really."

"What happens now?" Kayli asked.

"We'll take him back. Force the little shit to tell us where Mark is," Mac replied.

"Good. He deserves it. What about Abdul? I knew he looked shifty."

"Don't worry. I'll deal with him before the day is out. He's obviously forgotten that I know where he lives. We'll pick him up on the way back. With two of them there, one of them is bound to talk."

Giles joined them. "Are you all right?"

She shook her head. "Of course I'm not. We have to find Mark quickly. Remember my dreams, Giles."

"Don't worry. We'll have these pricks singing before daylight."

"But it could be too late to save him by then," Kayli said, swiping at the fresh tears rolling down her face.

Jacko and Bandy dragged the man towards them. They came to a halt in front of Kayli. She spat in the man's face. "You're despicable. May you rot in hell for what you've done."

He shouted back at her in his own language as Jacko and Bandy marched him to the car.

"Let's get back to the house," Jacko shouted over his shoulder.

"Wait. I need to check the vehicle for myself." She tore open the car doors to find three dead men: two in the front, one in the back, all with bullet holes in their foreheads. She rushed to the back of the car and opened the boot. It sprang open. Inside was a cache of weapons and ammunition. Giles looked over her shoulder then pushed her gently aside to retrieve the weapons.

"We can never have too much. We need to get out of here before reinforcements arrive."

"Where is he, Giles? Do you think they've killed him?"

"We'll find out soon enough. Let's go."

Giles placed the weapons in the back of Jacko's car, and they all squeezed into the vehicle. The decision had been made that they would take the rebel back to the house, then Mac and Bandy would go and pick up Abdul.

~ ~ ~

At the house, half an hour later, the two men were bound by rope and sitting on the floor in the middle of the room. Bandy had a towel in his hand, twisting and untwisting it in front of him. Mac brought the jerrycan of water closer. The two men glanced at each other then at Bandy and Mac.

"Which one of you is going to be first? Believe us, you will give us the information we need or die." Jacko sneered at the two trembling individuals.

"Our men will come. They will kill you if you harm us," the man who had pretended to be Mark said.

"We'll see about that. If they come, we'll be ready for them. We killed your men and sustained no casualties of our own, remember?"

The man's bravado wilted, and his head sank.

"Right, you're first, mouth almighty." Jacko gave the nod for Mac and Bandy to grab the man.

They positioned a small boulder on the floor and placed the man on top of it, the boulder pressing into his spine, then they draped the towel over his mouth and nose. Jacko unscrewed the jerrycan and emptied the water over the towel. The man tried to turn his head and kick out, but Giles was holding his legs firmly.

Kayli battled to hold back the bile burning her throat. She'd never witnessed any form of torture before. She abhorred it. However, she was eager for the men to suffer if it meant getting Mark back. The thoughts invading Kayli's mind sickened her. *Is this what soldiers had to contend with when they had to endure battle zones? Their characters changing at the flick of a switch?* She looked over at Abdul. He was shaking from head to foot, his eyes tightly squeezed shut. His lips moved as he mouthed a silent prayer. *Bloody hypocrite!*

Jacko stopped pouring the liquid and whipped the towel away from the man's face. "Ready to talk yet? Where are you keeping Mark, the Western man?"

The man shook his head in defiance despite his eyes being wide with fear. Jacko draped the towel over his face again and proceeded to pour the water. This time, he refused to remove the towel until he thought the man was close to death. Once the towel was withdrawn, the rebel spluttered and gasped to catch his breath, but still, he refused to talk. So Jacko kept up the pressure and draped the towel over the man's face again. He picked up a second jerrycan and proceeded to pour the water over the man's mouth and nose. Moments later, the man stopped struggling, and his body went limp.

Abdul yelled at the soldiers to stop and pointed a shaking hand at the blood covering the towel. Jacko motioned for Bandy and Mac to toss the man aside and grab Abdul. He tried to back away from them. "No, please, I tell you. Please, I have wife and children. We desperate for money. They pay me, order me to get you to library."

Jacko shook his head. "You knew you were leading us into a trap, and you expect us to forgive you for that?"

"I sorry. If you quick you can catch them."

"Who?"

"The men who transport your friend to Kabul. They left few hours ago."

Mac kicked his contact in the leg. "You bastard. *If* you have a family, your stupidity has just put them at risk."

"No, please, leave my family out of this," the man pleaded, clutching his hands together.

"You're the one who has involved them, not us. Where are the men taking him? Don't lie either. Remember, we know where you live."

"To secure place. I take you." He smiled and nodded eagerly.

"My take is we waterboard him, make sure he's telling us the truth now. I don't trust the weasel," Jacko said quietly to the others.

"I agree," Kayli surprised herself, uttering the words before anyone else responded.

Amused, Jacko ordered the men to take up their stations while he dragged a reluctant Abdul into position, the rock digging into his back.

He screamed. "Please, I tell truth this time. Don't do this. Think of my children."

Kayli leaned in close and snarled. "Tell us the truth and your family will be safe—you have our word. Where is he?"

"I told you. We catch them, if we go now," Abdul insisted, adding a little smile.

"We'll see if this changes your mind," Jacko warned as he placed the towel over Abdul's face. The man started crying and begging, but his words were swallowed up when the water began pouring over his nose and mouth. Jacko halted sooner than he had with the first man.

Abdul gasped for breath and pleaded with Jacko, "Please, I speak truth. I no want to die. My children need me. My wife is sick. I did it for money. You have to believe me."

Jacko again put the towel over the man's face and poured the water. Kayli sensed the man was telling the truth this time, but was there any way of really knowing if he was. She placed a hand over Jacko's to stop him. "I think he's telling the truth. If you kill him, we'll never see Mark alive again. We *have* to believe him."

Jacko scanned the room, searching for the other men's approval. One by one, they nodded their agreement to put a halt to the torture. Kayli sighed with relief as Jacko uncovered Abdul's face, and Mac and Bandy sat him upright. The man spluttered and gasped heavily.

"Take it nice and slowly," Jacko said. "We're done with you, Abdul. I swear, if you're lying to us..." He picked up the gun lying on the floor beside him and placed it to the man's forehead. "I'll take pleasure in killing you, then we'll return to your house and wipe out all of your family. You got that?"

The man snivelled. "Yes, I understand. Please, I no want to harm my family. I tell you only truth now."

"Good," Jacko said, patting the man on his shoulder. "Untie him—no wait, let's leave his hands and feet tied. We'll carry him out to the car. Looks like we're going to Kabul, folks."

"That's over four hours from here. We're going to need to top up the car first," Bandy said. "I think there's some diesel left in the yard. I'll do that now. You guys stay here until I give you the nod."

Bandy left the room and returned a few minutes later to give them the thumbs-up. Everyone piled into the car. Abdul was squeezed in between Mac and Giles. Kayli was against the door, the door handle digging into her thigh. *Great, nice comfortable journey ahead. It'll be worth it, though, if we can rescue Mark.*

The journey was conducted mostly in silence. Abdul was the only one to fall asleep.

"Sleeping beauty, he ain't!" Giles joked, trying to keep their spirits high.

Kayli chuckled and sighed heavily. She was tired, but the thought of falling asleep with a traitor in the car prevented her eyes from drooping. Dozens of questions ran through her mind. Would Abdul be able to take them to where the Taliban were keeping Mark? Would it turn out to be yet another trap? Could they save Mark before the Taliban got spooked and killed him?

CHAPTER FIFTEEN

Kayli felt stiff as well as tired when they arrived on the outskirts of Kabul. They had driven mostly through a vast desert to get there. Looking all around her, she could tell the area was still a war zone. Every building was either missing a corner or had hundreds of bullet holes in its façade. How could people live like this? They just got on with life apparently. Maybe it was pointless rebuilding the city with the Taliban and ISIS fighting it out for control.

"Someone give Sleeping Beauty a prod, will you?" Jacko called over his shoulder.

Both Giles and Mac elbowed the man heavily in the chest. He screamed out, and Kayli wasn't sure if it was because of fear or pain. "I not asleep."

"Glad to hear it. Where should we be heading now?" Jacko asked.

The man glanced out the window to get his bearings. "You want west of city."

"You'll need to give us more than that. Give us directions from here."

The man proceeded to tell them which roads to take. Some were main roads, and others were narrow side streets. Giles and Mac had the guns aimed out the windows at all times. Kayli felt like a sitting duck in her position next to the door, but she refused to let on to the others, as they had enough to deal with already.

Around thirty minutes later, Abdul shouted, "Stop. The cave is near here. We must approach on foot."

Silence filled the car for a moment or two as Jacko and his men surveyed the area. At only three in the morning, it was still dark. Any movement they made would be shielded by the night. There were no streetlights in this part of town.

"How are we going to play this then, Jacko?" Mac asked.

"I'm thinking."

"One of us needs to recce the area on foot, I'd say," Giles suggested.

"Where is the building?" Jacko asked Abdul.

He pointed ahead. "Down there, on left."

"I'll go," Mac volunteered. He opened the back door, slipped out of the car, and closed the door softly behind him. With his machine gun aimed and ready to fire, he slid along the side of the nearby buildings into the darkness. A full ten minutes passed before he returned.

"I think I've found it. There are two armed men on guard. Looks like an old wooden door they're guarding. I think I could make out a chunky padlock too."

"Good, sounds conceivable. We need to figure out how we're going to distract the men. The last thing we want to do is start a gun battle at this time of the morning," Jacko said.

"We could use Abdul as bait," Mac replied.

"What? Me? No, please, sir, not me. I no want trouble. I have..."

"Yeah, we know, a family to consider," Mac interrupted him. "Well guess what, dickhead? We've all got family to consider. Life sucks at times, right?"

Abdul's head dropped to his chest. He was clearly ashamed of the way he had begged. "I do it if you want," he mumbled.

Mac patted him on the shoulder. "Good man. I knew you'd see sense sooner or later." He cut the rope around Abdul's wrists and ankles.

"Okay, I think we need to split up. Mac and Giles, you go with Abdul. If he screws up, then shoot the bastard."

Abdul gasped and covered his heart with his hand. "I no screw up. I be good from now on. You trust me."

"You've got to earn our trust, man. This could be an ideal way to do that," Mac told him, a sneer tugging at his lips.

Abdul nodded profusely. "I do that. I promise. Don't let the men hurt me. I have family I need to care for."

"Will you fucking give it a break about your family, man. I've heard enough about them. You're lucky you're not dead by now after leading us into a trap. You fucking deserve to be." Mac sneered in the man's face before yanking him out of the vehicle.

Kayli grabbed Giles's forearm and pecked him on the cheek. "Please be careful."

"That's a given, sis. Stay in the car. Let Jacko and Bandy do what's necessary at the other end, but you remain in the car. Got that?"

"I hear you. Just take care of yourself. I can't believe we're so close."

"Keep the faith. We're not sure of that fact yet." Giles followed Abdul and Mac out of the car. Kayli watched them leave, her eyes straining through the darkness until they disappeared out of view.

"Kayli, get down. We're going to drive past the men," Jacko warned.

The car started up. Kayli lay flat on the back seat. They drove past at normal speed to avoid raising the guard's suspicions.

"Although heavily armed, they seem lightweight to me," Bandy said.

"I agree. They should be easy to take down. We'll pull over at the end of the street and double back. Kayli, you stay in the car. Lock yourself in. You hear me?" Jacko ordered.

"Okay, I won't disagree with you. Don't leave me hanging around, though. I'm eager to see Mark."

"We're aware of that. You do anything foolish, and you could jeopardise the mission."

Kayli sighed. "Grant me with some sense. I've learnt my lesson. You're in charge. I'll follow orders, I promise."

Jacko didn't respond. The engine died, and she heard Jacko and Bandy get out of the car. She quickly locked all the doors and looked out the back window at the men until they too disappeared into the darkness. She began chewing a fingernail. Time dragged by. Her gaze shifted from window to window, mindful that she needed to remain vigilant of what was going on around her.

All of a sudden, five figures approached the car. Recognising them, she unlocked the doors and sat forward in her seat. Giles opened the back door and shot in beside her. She tried to read the expression on his face, but it was impossible. Mac forced Abdul into the car then climbed in after him. Bandy and Jacko hopped in the front seats.

Kayli's heart was racing. "Jesus, will someone tell me what's going on? Where's Mark?"

Giles shook his head. "He wasn't there. The men were guarding an ammunition storage cave."

"Shit!" She reached across her brother and slapped Abdul across the face. "Where is he, you bastard?"

The man eyed her, defiance blazing in his eyes. "No woman should lay her hand on man."

"Tough. I just did, arsehole. Now tell me where Mark is?"

He hitched up a shoulder, his gaze boring into hers. "I thought he was there. I was wrong."

Kayli tried to scratch the man's eyes out, but Giles grabbed her wrists before she made contact. "He ain't worth it. He'll get his comeuppance. Don't worry about that."

She slumped back into her seat as tears of frustration and desperation slipped down her cheeks.

"He's around, Kayli. Just hang in there. We need another informant to find out where they're keeping him. Abdul says he knows a couple of men in the city who should be able to help him. We're going to see them now," Jacko told her.

The car started up, and she mumbled, "Great, you're still going to believe this piece of shit in spite of him leading you up the garden path, not once—but twice."

"Wind your neck in, sis. You ain't helping matters," Giles reprimanded her.

She folded her arms and gazed out the window, her own angry reflection making her flinch. The car pulled up outside a house a few minutes later. Mac and Jacko took Abdul with them and entered the house.

"Kayli, look, we're so near," Giles said. "Don't let your faith desert you now, not after we've come this far."

"Believe me, I'm trying not to let that happen. I feel so helpless, knowing how much Mark is suffering. I sense he's close. We just need to find him. I hate being reliant on this shitty weasel, though. He's caused us nothing but grief so far. I wouldn't trust a thing he says."

Giles shrugged and shook his head. "I hear what you're saying, but he's all we've got, love."

The door opened, and the men piled back into the car. "Nothing," Mac informed them.

"What now?" Giles asked.

"We have another address nearby to try. Point the way, Abdul," Jacko ordered.

The man gave them directions, and within minutes, they were pulling up outside another rundown house similar to the one they had stayed in when they arrived in Kandahar. Again, Mac and Jacko accompanied Abdul into the house. This time, they came running out a few moments later with good news.

"The bloke reckons Mark was moved again this evening to another cave close by. Abdul, give me the directions," Jacko demanded.

Abdul shouted out the directions that took them to the outskirts of the city. More rundown houses lined the dusty streets. In the distance, the sunrise was breaking over the desert.

"We need to make it snappy, guys. The sun's coming up," Kayli pointed out.

"We'll do it. Don't worry," Giles replied, winking at her.

Abdul directed them to a short road and said the cave they were after was at the end of that road. Kayli's mind whirled and pondered how this man knew the area so well when he lived in Kandahar. *Yes, he'd received the directions from one of his friends but...*

Jacko interrupted her thoughts. "Mac and Giles, you go ahead. We won't be able to drive past this time. Report back with your findings, and we'll go from there."

Her brother and Mac left the vehicle. Abdul remained in the car beside her. Her skin crawled as if a thousand cockroaches were feasting on her flesh. She hadn't known the man long, but she detested him. Whether he was genuine about his family or not, being mere inches away from him had a devastating effect on her that she'd never felt before. Maybe it was because she thought the man was toying with them. Had he been a suspect on a case back in Bristol, she would have clouted him one and put it down to resisting arrest, or at least ordered Dave to give him a good hiding.

It seemed an eternity before Mac and Giles returned. Breathlessly, Mac filled them in. "A similar scenario to last time. Two men guarding a large wooden door. It's going to be tricky to overcome them if we can't surprise them from both sides."

"Let me think about this for a moment..." Jacko rubbed his forehead with his hand.

"If I could make a suggestion...," Kayli said tentatively.

Jacko nodded. "I'm open to that. Shoot."

"I could distract them," she said.

"No way," Giles said immediately.

"Don't start pulling the big-brother act on me, Giles. Needs must on this one. I'll walk past and ask the way or something."

Giles ground his teeth and shook his head. "No. I won't allow you to do it."

"I'm inclined to agree with your brother. It's too dangerous. If these men recognise you as being a Westerner, there's no telling what they'd do to you. They despise Western women. It's drilled into them at an early age not to trust them," Jacko told her.

She flung her hands up in the air in frustration. "Then what are we going to do? It'll be sunrise soon, guys. We need to get a shift on if we're going to surprise these shits."

"We use Abdul to distract them," Mac said.

Abdul began to shake his head. "No, I not do it. These men no trust anyone, not just Western women."

Mac slapped him around the head. "You will do it, or I'll ring our boys back in Kandahar and tell them to round up your family and put them before a firing squad. It's your choice, mate."

"Okay, okay. What you want me do?" Abdul agreed reluctantly.

"Strike up a conversation. Get them to relax a little. That's when we'll attack," Jacko said.

"How?"

Mac poked his temple roughly. "Use this. Come on, Abdul, remember what I said. It'll only take a phone call from me."

"Okay. I thinking what I say. Stop the threats."

Mac glared at him.

"Mac, you and Bandy go with him. Stay back until you think you can strike. Have you got your knives handy?"

Mac nodded and patted his belt. "Yep, I'm all for slicing their throats open." He turned to Abdul. "Yours too if you step out of line again."

The man cowered from Mac. "I won't. You have my word."

Mac, Abdul and Bandy left the car.

Jacko sat forward in his seat to observe them as the darkness gave way to light. "Shit, they better hurry up. Sod it. Come on, Giles, I can't stand sitting around here."

"Please, let me come with you. I promise to behave," Kayli pleaded.

Giles sighed. "I'd rather have her with me, Jacko."

"Okay, don't do anything to make me regret my decision, Kayli. That's a warning."

Kayli nodded and smiled broadly. "I won't, I promise."

The three of them left the vehicle and used the shadows of the buildings for cover as they ran down the street to join the others. They heard a gunshot ahead of them and stopped briefly in their tracks until Jacko shouted, "Come on, let's shift it up a gear."

They surged forward and found the two guards propped up against the wall, both dead, their throats slit open. Lying ahead of them in the road was Abdul. He had a gunshot wound in his head and the blood was seeping from the hole.

"One of the fuckers shot him before he had the chance to open his mouth. Guess they realised he was up to something and decided to wipe him out," Mac said, eyeing his contact with a look of resignation.

"Pat them down. They must have a key for the lock," Jacko ordered.

Kayli gasped and stared at the door.

Giles swiftly ran to her side and flung an arm around her shoulders. "What is it?"

Her gaze met his, and she whispered, "It's the door in my dreams. He's in there... he has to be."

"Don't worry, Kayli. We've got this," Giles reassured her.

Bandy handed Jacko a key for the lock. He opened it and removed the rusty metal, tossing it aside in the road. He inched the door open. Beads of sweat broke out on Kayli's brow.

Giles squeezed her shoulder. "Stay strong, love."

Her palms were clammy, and she wiped them down her leggings. Her fear of confined spaces reared its ugly head when she least needed it.

"Watch there's not a booby trap inside, Jacko," Bandy shouted.

Jacko gave him a thumbs-up and eased the door open wider. "Shit!" he shouted and stepped back to address his men. "There are two cobras in there guarding him."

Mac laughed. "Is that all? I can deal with them. I have a python at home."

The other men stared at him as if he'd lost his mind. He squeezed past Jacko and stepped into the cave. Moments later, he emerged with a wicker basket in his hands. "They're safely tucked up in bed now. Maybe they would have been better using a couple of Rottweilers instead."

"Except they can't stand dogs in this country." Giles chuckled.

"Guys, can we stop with the crap and get in there and save Mark?" Kayli shoved Giles towards the cave.

"After you," Mac called out.

She shook her head. "I can't. I have a phobia of confined spaces."

"Crap. Okay, he's alive. However, you need to prepare yourself, Kayli," Mac warned.

"What the hell does that mean?" She rushed forward and pushed open the door. Her eyes took a little while to adjust to the dark within the cave. "Mark, baby, we're here."

"Kayli... Kayli, is that you?"

The sound of his voice was enough for her to forget all about her fears. She swiftly ran into the cave and knelt beside him. "Quick, get me some water." His lips were cracked almost to the point of bleeding. His hands were chained to a large ring in the wall above his head. He wore trousers but nothing else. His chest had deep gashes as if he had been whipped by the bastards, and his ribs were visible under his dirty skin.

Giles knelt beside her and passed her a water bottle. "Hello, mate. I see you've been hanging around, waiting for us to arrive," her brother joked.

His quip earned him a dig in the ribs from Kayli before she placed the bottle to her lover's lips.

When Mark nodded for her to stop, she lowered the bottle and ran a hand down his grubby cheek. He flinched at her touch.

"What's wrong?" she asked, searching his face for injuries.

"The bastards yanked out a couple of my back teeth," Mark replied, his voice sounding a little more like normal since his vocal cords had been moistened.

"Fuck. That's tough, mate," Giles said. "Never mind, at least it won't affect your smile."

Mark grinned. "That's a relief. Kayli would tear my nuts off if I didn't have a decent set of gnashers for the wedding."

She leaned forward and kissed him lightly on the lips. "Ain't that the truth?"

"Okay, lovefest over. Step aside Kayli. Let's rid him of these chains and get the fuck out of here before anyone else turns up," Jacko ordered.

Kayli left Mark's side and stood guard at the entrance as the men unshackled him. Even though her heart felt much lighter now that they'd found him, she doubted if she would feel a hundred percent happy until they were safely back on the plane heading home.

She almost jumped out of her skin when a pair of arms circled her waist. Turning, she saw Mark smiling down at her. He whispered, "Can we go home now?"

Kayli kissed him. The other men cheered before Jacko broke up the party by ordering them to get back to the car.

"Where do we go from here?" Kayli asked once they were all squashed into the car.

Jacko held up a finger, telling her to be patient, and called someone on his mobile. "That's brilliant. We'll be there in fifteen to twenty." He ended the call and swivelled in his seat to talk to Mark. "I've arranged for an army doctor to check you out, mate. I doubt you'll be given the all-clear to travel until they've done that."

"I understand. Any chance we can stop off and get some grub on the way? My fuel tank is empty. As soon as that's replenished, I know I'm going to feel tons better." He smiled at Kayli and placed her hand to his lips.

"No problem, mate. We'll make a slight detour up ahead," Jacko replied.

Kayli held hands with Mark, unable to let him go until they reached a small market area. Bandy and Mac left the vehicle to gather supplies. Everyone was hungry, but that was an understatement to what Mark must have been feeling.

"Hey, you need to slow down and savour your food," Kayli warned him.

Mark tore into the chicken and shrugged at Kayli. "It's been a couple of weeks since I've had a proper meal. They fed me on scraps, tortured me by eating their own meals in front of me."

"The bastards. You'll never go through that again, Mark. You're safe now."

With sticky lips, he kissed her on the cheek before tucking into the chicken again. No matter how many warnings they gave him about slowing down, it was obvious that wasn't going to happen.

~ ~ ~

They arrived at the military base in Kabul and ushered Mark in to see the doctor. Giles told Jacko and his men to head off, but they insisted on staying around until Mark had been given the all-clear.

Kayli was by Mark's side during his examination. "So, what's the prognosis, Doctor? Will he live?"

The doctor smiled. "There are a few more tests I'd like to run, possibly keep him in overnight just in case he relapses. However, I don't think that's likely to happen. His blood pressure and heart are near normal, remarkable considering what he's been through. I'll get one of the nurses to clean up his wounds and check in on him later this evening."

Mark tutted and puffed out his cheeks. "Hey, Doc, I was hoping to get out of this shithole today. Umm... by that, I mean the country, not the hospital."

Kayli patted his hand and smiled. "Another twenty-four hours isn't going to hurt, Mark."

"I suppose."

The doctor nodded. "Twenty-four hours maximum, I swear. I wouldn't be doing my job properly if I released you before we had a chance to study the test results. You're safe here."

"Thank you, Doctor." Kayli shook the doctor's hand. When he left the room, she hugged Mark tightly. "He's right. What's another twenty-four hours? It'll give Giles time to organise the trip back home."

Mark smiled. "You're right. I'm glad you're here, babe."

"So am I." A nurse appeared. "I'll leave you in safe hands and bring the guys up to date." She kissed him on the cheek and left the room.

The four men were pacing the hallway, eager to hear the news.

"Well? What did the doc say, sis?"

Kayli walked over to her brother, her eyes misting up with tears. "He's not prepared to give him the all-clear for another twenty-four hours. He has a few tests to run, but he doesn't see them being a problem."

Giles let out a relieved sigh and gathered her in his arms. "Thank God."

She pulled out of his grasp and turned to face the other men. She placed a hand over her chest as she spoke, "Guys, I want to thank you with all my heart for helping us to free Mark. We couldn't have done it without you."

"Aww shucks," Mac said, "does this mean you'll be putting us on your Christmas-card list from now on, Kayli?"

She laughed. "Ever the wise guy. Hey, I owe you all a steak dinner."

Jacko, looking serious, took a step towards her and reached for her hand. He held it between both of his. "It was our pleasure, little lady. We never leave a man behind. Giles has our number. Let us know when the arrangements have been made to take you home."

"We will. Thanks again, guys. You're genuine heroes in my eyes."

Bandy winked at her. "Hey, you're not so bad yourself, love. Not many wives or girlfriends would leave Blighty to fly out here to rescue their man."

"I wouldn't have dreamt of doing that if Giles hadn't agreed to accompany me. I'm so grateful to you all."

Giles slung an arm around her shoulder. "I couldn't let my kid sister down."

Jacko cleared his throat. "We better get a shift on. Ring us with an update, mate. It was good to see you again."

Kayli and Giles hugged each of the men before they set off down the hallway. "I can see why you and Mark loved being in the army so much now."

"Yeah, maybe it's something we should both consider going back to in the near future."

Her head snapped round to look at him. "I hope you're winding me up?"

His face was deadly serious for a second or two, then he punched her in the arm. "Of course I am. Glad we managed to get him back, love. He seems okay. Not sure if that's because you're here, though."

"I'm so relieved and grateful to you guys for your support. I guess we'll have to see how Mark recovers over the coming weeks."

"There's one good thing."

Kayli frowned. "There's more than one, but what are you getting at?"

"He didn't even notice you'd chopped your hair off."

Kayli chuckled. "I'm not sure whether to be upset or thankful about that."

~ ~ ~

The hospital had a couple of spare beds for Giles and Kayli to use that night, and once Kayli's head hit the pillow, she slept soundly for the first time in weeks. After the doctor gave Mark the all-clear the next morning, they boarded the plane and flew back to England via Turkey.

Giles had volunteered to ring their parents to share the good news. She was overjoyed to see her mum and dad waiting for them in the arrivals lounge, along with Annabelle and Bobby. It was a tearful reunion for everyone.

Her mum and dad insisted on taking them all out for a meal on the way home. Despite wanting to get reacquainted with each other properly, Kayli and Mark agreed. It turned out to be a wonderful family evening and proved to Kayli once again, how lucky she was to have such a caring and loving support network.

EPILOGUE

Over the next week, Kayli doted on Mark. It had taken nearly losing him forever for her to realise how much she loved him. He truly was her soulmate. Reluctantly, she kissed him goodbye and returned to work on the Monday of the following week.

The team made a genuine fuss over her as soon as she walked into the incident room. At just gone nine, she received a call summoning her for a meeting with DCI Davis.

Tentatively, she opened the door to the DCI's office. "Safe to come in, ma'am?"

Davis gave her a sincere welcoming smile and gestured for Kayli to join her. Pushing her paperwork aside, she folded her arms. "Well, that's something I wasn't expecting to see."

Kayli's brow furrowed. "What's that, ma'am?"

"You with short hair. How did that come about? Actually, I have a spare ten minutes. I want to know *all* about your mission."

It was the last thing Kayli had expected to hear when she'd stepped into the room. Once she'd recounted every detail of her adventure, DCI Davis was left shaking her head. "That's it in a nutshell. We swooped in and saved him."

"You're amazing. A seriously ballsy character, Kayli Bright. It's an absolute privilege to have you on my team."

She felt her cheeks warm. "Thank you. I must say I'm pretty proud of what went down myself, but it wouldn't have been possible without Giles and his mates. If they hadn't joined up with us, I dread to think what the outcome would have been."

"Then don't think about it. I'm so pleased for you. I'm also impressed that you managed to do it within your allocated two-week holiday."

They both laughed.

"The consequences were always prominent in my mind if I didn't succeed, ma'am," Kayli admitted.

"That's bullshit, Inspector, and you know it. Okay, now bugger off. You have a bit of catching up to do, I believe. You'll be pleased to know that Dave has coped admirably in your absence."

"I never doubted it for an instant, ma'am." She left her seat and walked towards the door.

"By the way. I've arranged for us to have a drink after work to celebrate you all solving the Sarah Abel case. We never did get a chance to do that before you swanned off on your little adventure."

"Oh? When?"

"This evening, at five o'clock smart at the pub across the road, as usual."

Kayli's heart sank. She knew that by the end of the day, all she would want to do was rush home to be in Mark's arms again. Their time together over the last week had been very special, and she had hoped to continue spoiling him once she was back at work. "I'll look forward to it, ma'am. Mind if it's only a brief get-together?"

"Not at all. See you later. Oh and you'll be pleased to know that I had a word with Gary Young, told him we'd caught the real killer. He accepted my apology and agreed to drop any charges against you that he was contemplating making."

"That's a relief. Thanks, ma'am."

Kayli rushed back to the incident room to inform the rest of the team and announce the DCI's plans for that evening. They all seemed excited by the prospect, which only made her thoughts about returning home quickly seem selfish.

While she was caught up on the paperwork piled high on her desk, Dave filled her in on the couple of minor cases the team had solved in her absence.

At four fifty-five, DCI Davis poked her head around Kayli's office door, startling her. "Leave that, and yes, that's an order. We have a celebration to attend."

Together, the team entered the pub. Kayli was taken aback when she saw her family standing in the pub's banquet suite. "Hey, what are you guys doing here?" Her heart sank when she looked around and noticed that everyone was there except for Mark.

The family beamed at her but said nothing. Suddenly, Bryan Adams's voice flooded through the speakers. Her breath caught in her throat. *Everything I Do* was Kayli and Mark's tune. She shook her head, puzzled. She saw Annabelle reach for something from the chair behind her. It was a beautiful cream wedding dress.

Kayli gasped. "That's beautiful, but I don't understand..."

The crowd before her parted to reveal Mark, standing alongside a woman in her fifties. Kayli's legs faltered as she walked slowly towards him. He was wearing a grey wedding suit and looked devilishly handsome.

"Kayli Bright, will you do me the honour of being my wife?"

Tears slipped onto her cheeks. "Of course."

She was suddenly swept up into a tornado of activity. Annabelle and her mother whisked her off to the ladies' toilet, where they tore off her work suit and dressed her in the bridal gown. Annabelle then applied her makeup while her mother tried to do something fancy with her short hair. Everything happened in a blur, and within fifteen minutes, she was standing alongside Mark as the wedding celebrant conducted the ceremony. She didn't even remember uttering the words "I do," but she must have, because now she was displaying a wedding band on her left hand.

The last two weeks her emotions had been on a rollercoaster ride, but this truly was the icing on the cake. To be Mrs. Mark Wren was all she'd ever wanted, and if it hadn't been for her steely determination to bring him home, she doubted they would be standing here now, celebrating her dream.

THE END

NOTE TO THE READER

Dear Reader,

Love conquered all in the end, for Kayli and Mark. They're a very special couple.

Are you ready for the next case?

A missing person case is on the agenda for Kayli and her team. With a suspect on the run she'll need to keep her wits about her. This story will keep you glued to the page, I guarantee it.

Grab your copy today.

http://melcomley.blogspot.co.uk/p/murderous-betrayal.html

I'd like to take this opportunity to thank you for your support.

M A Comley

Sprinkle a little fairy dust in my direction by considering leaving a review if you will.

Printed in Great Britain
by Amazon